"We should kiss and make up too," Dave said.

"What for? Gwen asked, her voice trembling slightly.

"For the last time we kissed." His smile glimmered, then faded. "You haven't forgotten, have you? I know I never called you back. . . ."

"I didn't blame you. A little champagne, some dancing—it got away from us, that's all," she said.

"It wasn't the champagne."

"It was."

"One way to find out," he dared her softly.

She sensed it before she felt it, his face closing in, his mouth speaking, then breathing a scant inch away, then the brush of his lips.

Her eyes were closed. They shouldn't have been. Closed was a sign of surrender, a way of saying *Take me, I trust you*. . . .

"That didn't hurt, did it?" he asked, then kissed her again quickly. "I turned you on like a light bulb once. You're afraid to admit it."

"One kiss," she said, trying to scoff at him. "Four years ago."

He smiled, and she knew he saw through her denial. "You're burning still. . . ."

WHAT ARE *LOVESWEPT* ROMANCES?

They are stories of true romance and touching emotion. We believe those two very important ingredients are constants in our highly sensual and very believable stories in the *LOVESWEPT* line. Our goal is to give you, the reader, stories of consistently high quality that may sometimes make you laugh, sometimes make you cry, but are always fresh and creative and contain many delightful surprises within their pages.

Most romance fans read an enormous number of books. Those they truly love, they keep. Others may be traded with friends and soon forgotten. We hope that each *LOVESWEPT* romance will be a treasure—a "keeper." We will always try to publish

LOVE STORIES YOU'LL NEVER FORGET
BY AUTHORS YOU'LL ALWAYS REMEMBER

The Editors

Loveswept ® 536

Terry Lawrence
For Lovers Only

BANTAM BOOKS
NEW YORK · TORONTO · LONDON · SYDNEY · AUCKLAND

FOR HERB AND AMY AND ARROWHEAD

FOR LOVERS ONLY
A Bantam Book / April 1992

If you would be interested in receiving protective vinyl
covers for your Loveswept books, please write to this address
for information:

Loveswept
Bantam Books
P.O. Box 985
Hicksville, NY 11802

ISBN 0-553-44188-4

Published simultaneously in the United States and Canada

PRINTED IN THE UNITED STATES OF AMERICA

OPM   0 9 8 7 6 5 4 3 2 1

One

The phone trilled. Exhausted, her head stuffed with numbers, statistics, and formulas—even in her sleep—Gwen struck out at the offending appliance, bobbling the clattering receiver across the pillow. She answered by sheer force of habit. "Gwen Stickert, may I help you?"

"Wake up. I have some bad news. It's Charlotte and Robert."

"Mother?" Eyes wide, Gwen clutched the sheet to her chest as her heart slammed against her rib cage and her skin went cold. She knew she'd always remember that crack in the ceiling, the clock reading 12:01. "What happened?"

Her mother answered tightly. "They've gone to the cottage."

"Huh?" Gwen sat up so fast, she nearly knocked her glasses off the nightstand with the phone cord. She saved her teacup, the alarm clock, and the hippo figurine, but *Churchill: The Last Lion* hit the floor with a thud, revealing a neat outline of dust where the book had sat for weeks. After reading one hundred pages covering approximately four days in the great man's life, all she had to do was look at it to fall asleep.

Six weeks of intense studying for her CPA exam

was another excuse for her exhaustion, although that didn't stop her from automatically wiping the dust away at the sound of her mother's voice.

"Are you all right, darling? What was that noise?"

"What about Charlotte and Robert?" Gwen asked, finally clearing away the cobwebs in her head.

"They've gone to Lake Arrowhead. Robert wants the cottage in the divorce, and Charlotte got the brilliant idea of moving in to prevent him from taking it. I want you to go up there and see they don't kill each other, or worse, start breaking things."

Gwen sighed and sank back against a pillow gone flat. One of these days she was going to treat herself to a fat, fluffy one-hundred-percent eiderdown pillow— one of these days when she stopped playing family policeman, counselor, mediator, and all-around referee. "I'll find my striped shirt and whistle and leave in the morning."

"No need to get sarcastic, darling. Just go."

"Gram! Any late bingo winnings to report?"

"This is serious, Dave. It's about your brother Robert."

Dave clutched the receiver. He purposely relaxed his grip. No sense overreacting until he knew exactly what was going on. "Is he okay?"

"He's insisting on getting the cottage in the divorce decree."

"Some cottage." It was a three-story glass chalet in the San Bernadino Mountains approximately three hours east of L.A. They'd bought it right after their honeymoon with the proceeds from one of Charlotte's screenplays. But, as lawyer Robert would quickly point out at this stage in their stormy marriage, California was a community property state. They either divided it right down the middle, or they compromised. "Why doesn't one take the house in Long Beach and one take the cottage?"

"Don't be sensible, dear, they're divorcing. People divorcing are never sensible."

"Kind of like people in love."

"Don't be cynical either."

After spending six straight hours bent over his drafting table, Dave had already been jolted out of his concentration minutes earlier by the slamming of a car door, a predictable hazard when one rented an apartment over a garage. To be honest, he'd been itching for just such a distraction.

His back was aching, his eyelids felt scoured with beach sand, and his hand was cramped from holding a pen. The illustrations for *Amazon Women Warriors, Vol. I, Captured!* were so much Beatrix Potter. If he didn't get some life into them, he'd be drawing girdle ads for the Saturday insert.

"So why am I honored with this update from the war zone? Notifying next of kin?"

"I want you to go up to the cottage and keep your brother and sister-in-law from committing any mayhem that might get in the papers."

"In other words, wipe up the blood or pick up the broken china."

"That's more like it, dear."

The atmosphere at the Lake Arrowhead chalet was suspiciously hushed, as if the shouting had died with his car engine. Reluctant to stick his head inside until he was convinced there were no flying missiles. Dave shouted from the doorway, "Where's my favorite brother and sister-in-law?"

There was no sound. No bodies either. Dave heaved a sigh of relief as he finished inspecting the house. Since Robert's things were neatly stacked in the downstairs bunk room, Dave tossed his duffel bag in there. Poking his head in the master suite upstairs, he found ample evidence of Charlotte's mercurial nature; clothes, books, and talismans were scattered high and low.

Hearing a car outside, Dave stepped onto the side porch deck as a rusty tangerine Volvo slid into the drive. *Gwen.*

He hadn't expected Charlotte's sister to be there. He rubbed the stubble on his chin, instantly wishing he'd shaved before leaving town, second-guessing his shirt, his hair, his common sense.

Around Gwen he always felt like a beachcomber, a bum, some footloose college kid on a spring-break bender. The chin, the chinos, and the tattered duffel bag by the door weren't going to change her opinion of him this visit. He wondered for a second why it mattered what she thought. Except it did. Every time.

She waved through the dusty windshield.

He lifted a palm grown itchy and dry and felt his heart rev like a showroom Porsche.

"Howdy!" she called when the clamor of her car engine running on faded.

Kicking open the door, she eased past the steering wheel with an armload of books and a crushed fast-food bag under her arm.

Dave leaned on the open door, waiting in vain to be handed something. Hyper-efficient, Gwen never did two things at once when three would do.

"I wasn't expecting a welcoming committee," she said with a gasp.

"How about an ambulance brigade?"

Her eyes grew wide and she glanced at the cottage. "They haven't!"

"Kidding," he amended quickly. "Nobody's here."

"How's it look?"

"No blood. No smoking guns."

"That's something to be thankful for." Sighing, Gwen sank to the edge of the car seat and swung her purse strap up her arm, catching the shoulder harness instead. While she extricated herself from that, Dave squinted at the light shimmering on her hair.

She had an unremarkable face, if perfect hearts were unremarkable. A handful of freckles sprinkled across her nose matched the amber of her straight fine hair and eyes the color of caramel. Glasses rimmed with thin tortoiseshell frames emphasized her wide eyes. Unlike Charlotte, she didn't turn her lashes into mascara spikes or ring her eyes with kohl.

Charlotte was striking and emotive; Gwen was easy to look at, easy to be with. Soft-spoken, levelheaded, she plotted her life on graph paper and thought before she answered.

She also kissed like a dew-bestrewn fairy princess awakened from a spell.

Dave blinked, wondering what had brought that thought on.

He knew all too well. Once upon a time, he'd been a wild and crazy twenty-two, looking for a good time and a fun-loving woman at Charlotte and Robert's wedding reception. Leading a tipsy and uncharacteristically daring Gwen onto the dance floor, he'd kissed her. Her taste, her touch, her tongue, had damn near knocked his socks off.

So he'd gotten her phone number. And he'd never called. It had been typical of him at the time.

He wondered if she even remembered. And if he'd ever forget. The way she'd avoided him since, ought to tell him something—like *give up.*

Springing back into action, Gwen piled her miscellany on the hood of the car, bumping the door shut with some nifty hip action. The car shook with a tin can clang as flakes of rust floated onto the driveway. Oblivious, Gwen adjusted her glasses with her pinky. "So it's gotten that bad." She sighed. "Who'd have thought four years together could lead to this?"

"At least the wedding was pleasant."

"To be perfectly honest, they were sniping even then."

"Charlotte arrived with a biker escort. Can you blame Robert for getting ticked?" Dave asked.

"Wasn't that why he married her?" She laughed. "Drama, excitement, surprise?"

"It *was* an exciting evening. Especially the reception."

"Mmm," she replied noncommittally, studying the mountain range in the distance as if some condo company had erected it since the last time she'd been there. She wasn't about to join him in happy reminiscence of that reception, and he knew why. The Kiss.

"Late-night phone call?" he asked instead.

"Mother. You?"

"Gram. Doesn't want violence."

"We gave them a complete set of china for the wedding. Mother wants it to stay that way."

Dave chuckled low, slinging an arm casually across her shoulders, encouraging her with a swift tug to look up at him. His heart stopped when she did. She was five-two and pear-shaped, he six-two and built like a rail fence stood on end. That didn't stop him from touching her every chance he got, with pats, contact, hugs. Gwen needed hugs. "And what does Gwen want?"

"Peace and quiet," she answered flatly. "Some uninterrupted study time so I can pass the CPA exam."

"Thought you took that once."

"Thanks for reminding me."

"Flunked out, huh?"

"There's some salt in that sack. How about sprinkling it on the wound?"

He gave her another hug. "Knowing you, you'll beaver away at it until you pass. You'll get it. Don't worry."

"Thanks. I guess." She grimaced, listening to a car speeding up the winding road. "Think that's them?"

Dave was sure it was. That's why he took the chance. His reputation as the exuberant kid brother gave him a right to indulge in the unexpected, and an excuse to lift Gwen off her feet in a bear hug, whispering urgently in her ear. "Get out while you can. The roads are still open, the moon isn't full, and I can get you some garlic to wrap around your neck." He planted a kiss on her neck for good measure.

She playfully pounded him on the back. "Put me down."

"Put-downs are an art around here. You're playing with experts."

As usual, her look was pure good-natured tolerance. "Not you, too, I hope."

"Never me." It came out more sincerely than he'd intended. Her indulgent smile faltered. He almost said, "Hey, don't take me seriously." But that had never been a problem between him and Gwen.

She was eight years older than he. For some reason, he got the idea the age difference bothered her. Perhaps because she never let him forget it. And she never *ever* took him seriously.

The car sped by without stopping.

Gwen pushed her glasses firmly up her nose with her thumb, a signal fun time was over. "Think they'll need both of us to referee this spat?"

Already she was looking for a way out. He caught the way she rubbed her neck, as if contemplating the long drive back to L.A., or the kiss he'd dropped there.

Dave immediately scooped her books under one arm and headed toward the house. "Stick around, this could be a two-man job. I've already stashed my easel in the loft. Thought I'd turn this into a working vacation." He snuck in a plug for his hardworking, ambitious ways. Not that she'd believe it.

He hadn't missed that little frown line between her brows as she'd glanced at his Hawaiian shirt; cockatiels and lizards climbing horizontally across his chest in a riot of black, green, and pink. Her smile got very sweet, and Dave got a tight sensation in his chest, afraid she was going to pat him on the head.

"Still drawing comic books?" she asked.

"We prefer the term 'illustrating,' it's more, uh—"

"Illustrious?"

"Yep." He held open the cottage door.

"So this is the scene of the crime-to-be," she murmured, entering the cool darkness.

"There's some stuff splattered on the wall of the kitchen. It isn't blood or remains, I checked."

"Please." She shuddered. "Think the neighbors might have heard them arguing and had them both hauled off to jail?"

"Now there's a second happy thought."

"What's the first?" she asked.

"We're alone at last," he said with a leer, waggling his brows.

"Very funny," she muttered.

Not exactly the response he'd had in mind.

She crossed the living room without a backward glance and stood below the two-story wall of glass, peering at the towering pines outside and the vaulted wooden ceiling over them. Her head was back, all he had to do was lean down and skim his mouth over her hair, inhaling strawberry-scented shampoo and tasting—

"It's like living at the top of the world," she said softly. "Treetops, mountaintops. Think they have aspirin at the top of the world?" Practical Gwen.

"Whatever my lady desires shall be my command." Dave bowed with a flourish and headed for the master bedroom to check.

Outside, brakes screeched on the drive and a door slammed.

"They're baaack," he crooned.

Gwen laughed in spite of herself, and Dave's heart thumped at the sound. She lit up when she smiled. He remembered that. There were times he damn near cherished it—like now, when she looked so tired. He'd already given her several hugs. The lady needed a lot more. Obviously, she worked too hard, and with the exam coming up, she'd been working even harder.

Almost as obvious, Dave thought with a pang of exasperation, was the fact that she had no one in her life to notice how tired she was. People needed an escape from their responsibilities. She could have it there, with him. A peaceful retreat only sparring spouses and slamming car doors could mar.

Dave joined Gwen at the stained glass window beside the front door, surveying their respective siblings. "No mortal wounds that I can see," he murmured. "Nice to have a nurse on hand just in case."

"An accountant."

"That'll come in handy for damage estimates." He sidled closer, bumping her leg with his. "Will you bandage me if I get hurt in the crossfire?"

"Sorry, Dave, forgot the first aid kit," she replied dryly. "No playing doctor for us."

"I was getting my hopes up."

"Sounds like your hormones to me. We're supposed to be the adults here, remember?"

"Counting me in that company?"

"Provisionally."

He struggled to keep the irritation out of his voice. "I don't want to sound like I'm bragging, but most women leap at a chance to come to my place. You just put me in it."

She gave him a pat on the arm. It was just as bad as a pat on the head.

"Dave, when I'm going to step between two angry lions, I don't need a puppy nipping at my heels. Behave."

With that she turned the doorknob and stepped out on the porch to greet Charlotte and Robert.

Dave hesitated on the porch steps. *Puppy!* He was twenty-six to her thirty-four. Four years had passed since the wedding, and she'd given him no credit at all for getting older. In fact, he seemed to age backward in her estimation. "Get any younger than this, and my voice'll change again," he muttered, girding himself for battle.

He stepped down to the drive, speculating for a moment on who the real opponents were, Robert and Charlotte, or he and Gwen.

"My sister!" Charlotte threw herself into Gwen's embrace, surrounding her in pleated sleeves of ebony chiffon. "I knew you'd come," she cooed, "I need your support."

"She needs something," Robert stage-whispered to his brother. "Valium would be first on my list."

Gwen gave him a frown and launched into her speech. "Sorry I dropped in out of the blue, you two, but I have so much studying to do. My boss gave me some time off; accounting is pretty dead this time of year."

"Is it?" Charlotte asked politely. "And what about your social life, hon?"

As if one dead thing led directly to another, Gwen thought. It wasn't a question she wanted to answer with Dave standing right there. He seemed to view her as some kind of maiden aunt—coltishly flirting with her at every opportunity, teasing, joking. If he ever suspected the tremors he evoked in her simply by walking into a room, he'd probably run the other way—or laugh out loud.

Which was one excellent reason for keeping her hormones in check and her daydreams rated PG wherever brother-in-law's brother was concerned. And keeping Charlotte off the subject of romance. "Where can I unpack my stuff?"

"We have the main floor, darling," Charlotte replied, leading the way.

"I'll sleep downstairs, then."

"I meant you and me. The main floor is mine. Robert gets the cellar."

"The walk-out lower level," Robert corrected. "With the VCR and the wet bar. We'll camp out on the bunk beds like when we were kids, Dave."

"I was the kid. You were in college most of the time."

"That's what happens when you get into law school at sixteen."

Charlotte flounced toward the master bedroom with Gwen's suitcase. "Let's get out of here before he starts recounting his SAT scores!" The door slammed.

In a move he'd probably patented, Robert shook Dave's hand and gave him a simultaneous shoulder jab. The questioning wouldn't start just yet. "Good to see you, bro."

Clad in his usual cardigan and bow tie, Robert looked deceptively low-key for a tenacious civil rights lawyer who played best to the court of public opinion. In that respect, Charlotte's flamboyance had definitely rubbed off.

"My humble abode is your humble abode," he announced.

Overhearing, Charlotte poked her head out of the master bedroom off the living room. "*Your* humble abode? Not yet, buster."

"Ah, the little woman." Robert smirked.

Dave knew that look. And the icy sarcasm. Although he felt disloyal thinking it, his older brother could give quick wit a bad name.

If Robert's courtroom tactics involved slicing someone into neat cubes of logic, Charlotte was another story altogether. She did the gypsy curse scene to a turn: eyes ringed with mascara, black hair teased to six inches on every side of her head. She looked like Cher with her finger in a socket. Tragedy and melodrama were her métier. She dressed for maximum effect; a black chiffon ensemble wafted around her.

"In mourning?" Dave asked with a grin.

"For my life," she replied in a low, smoky voice. "For my marriage, which once held so much promise and now . . . ashes . . . all ashes. Oh, David, I'm so glad you're here." She gripped his shoulders, long red nails digging into his Hawaiian shirt.

Robert rolled his eyes.

Whipping her head around, Charlotte glowered at her husband, silently daring him to say anything, anything at all.

It was kind of like standing between a match and a very short fuse, Dave mused. He scanned the room for deadly weapons as Robert pierced him with that witness-box glare.

"And why are *you* here, little brother?"

Dave gave him his best don't-look-at-me shrug.

"Just thought I'd drive up to the mountains for awhile. L.A. this time of summer—well, fill in the complaint."

"Hot? Thick? Smoggy?" Charlotte offered.

"Congested, stultifying?" Robert suggested.

"So do me one better, Mister Hotshot Lawyer," Charlotte said stiffly.

"I only said—"

"You always say. If he doesn't get in the first word, he has to have the last. Tell me I'm right, David."

"Tell her she's nuts, Dave."

Dave edged his way toward Gwen. "Care to make a call here?"

Smoothly and tactfully, Gwen came to his defense. "Everybody's right—L.A. is miserable this time of year."

"Solomon couldn't have said it better," Dave murmured, giving her a wink.

An uncomfortable moment of silence descended. Uncannily, Charlotte's head tilted at the same angle as Robert's as they both studied the interlopers. Gwen found herself resisting moving closer to Dave.

Charlotte was the first to break the ice. "I *knew* you'd be here when I needed you," she declared, crossing the room with arms outstretched, tugging Gwen away from Dave. "The idea came to me last night. It was as if lightning had struck."

"That explains the hair," Robert muttered.

"You came to give me emotional support," she retorted, voice rising, "Something I've had so seldom, I've almost forgotten what it is. Like a tree in the desert, doomed to never bear fruit."

"But plenty of fruitcake," Robert mumbled.

"Maybe I should unpack my gear," Dave intervened, drawing Robert toward the lower level.

Robert grudgingly followed him below. "I've got the downstairs staked out," he announced importantly.

"With tripwires?" Dave bit his tongue. Tumbling the contents of his duffel bag onto the upper bunk, he cranked open a window. "Do you and Charlotte ever call time out? This is too nice a day to be arguing."

"Napoleon didn't cancel Waterloo because the weather was good."

"Maybe he should have." Dave ran a hand over the sun-warmed sheets of the upper bunk. The light slanted at a bewitching angle this time of day, subtle, suggestive. He pictured it highlighting a woman's skin, a cool woman on warm sheets. Gwen at that barbecue a couple of years back, for instance, laughing gaily—until he'd walked out to the pool.

She'd immediately found ten things to do, from dicing coleslaw to whipping up potato salad for sixty. Fortunately, Dave loved the stuff and found himself returning for seconds, thirds, fourths, and fifths. He'd even gotten her to laugh at a lame joke about Mr. Potatohead.

She was laughing still. At him. *Puppy!*

"Do you think she'll be trouble?" Robert asked.

She had him tied in 'nots' already. "Which one?" Dave responded.

"Gwen. I already know the trouble Charlotte can cause. She wants to clean me out."

"Be serious."

"She called in an accountant, didn't she?"

"Gwen? Their mother did the calling."

"That's *her* story."

"Gwen doesn't lie," Dave told him.

"Whoa. That *Dungeons and Dragons* chivalry's rubbing off, bro. Women stick together at times like this. We've gotta do the same." Hearing Dave's grumbled reply, Robert switched tactics. "I know you like her."

"Gwen buys me sweaters at Christmas and that's about it."

"You wear them constantly."

In fact, seconds earlier Dave had been sorting through his stuff looking for one to slip into. Mountain air was chilly. Thanks to Robert, he'd have to stick with the Hawaiian shirt Gwen pretended not to wince at.

Hardworking, goal-oriented, nose-to-the-grindstone Gwen. None of those terms had ever applied to him. So why didn't he take the hint? Robert and Charlotte were case studies in what mixing opposites led to.

Gwen treated him as if he were an overeager kid. Maybe it was time she met the man he'd become.

He stuffed the sweater back into his bag. A few more wrinkles would do it good.

Two

Gwen heard whistling in the kitchen. *Dave.* She fluffed her straight-arrow hair, ticked a fingernail against the stem of her glasses, and glanced in the gilded mirror beside the fireplace. Any new wrinkles and she'd qualify for A.A.R.P.

Lately they'd been cropping up like cracked earth during a drought. She'd begun studying her mother's face the way fortune tellers read palms, seeing her future as a veritable Etch-a-Sketch of aging. "You're thirty-four," she reminded herself, "wrinkles are perfectly normal." And perfectly dreadful.

She plastered on a smile anyway, cringed at the lines that sprang to life, and crossed the living room to the dining alcove. An aisle bounded by counters and cabinets formed the kitchen. In the middle of it, Dave sang lustily, his baritone bouncing off the tile walls.

"'This floor is mine, God gave this floor to me.'" He turned as she entered, and winked.

"Like parting the Red Sea, it'd be a miracle if we got these two sorted out," Gwen said.

"Or a fairy tale."

"Your territory, I believe. I like what makes sense, what adds up."

"Which means?"

"I have a suggestion to make."

"Be as suggestive as you want." He leaned a hip against the stove and smiled.

Her heart melted like the pat of butter in the pan—but not her professional demeanor. "I'm proposing an alliance."

"I'd prefer a misalliance." He raised his sandy brows in invitation.

"Seriously now." She squelched the sinking sensation that he *was* serious—it felt too much like hope. "We don't need four people biting one another's heads off."

"Or nipping at one another's heels?"

She sheepishly tucked a strand of hair behind her ear. It instantly shimmied free. "Sorry about that. Long drive. The way I see it, either we avoid taking sides, or before you know it we'll all be at one another's throats."

"So we team up," he said. "Dave and Gwen: menders of marital discord, fixers of fickle affairs."

"Somebody's gotta keep a clear head. On a beach, those two would fight over who had the better grain of sand."

"You know what they say, 'Life's a beach!'"

She laughed. Damn, he was sweet. And sharp. It was a good combination for a salsa, she thought wryly, the kind that added spice to everything it touched. He made her mouth water and her eyes widen—when she wasn't extremely careful. "Maintaining a sense of humor is a good idea too. Under the circumstances."

"Under *any* circumstances," he insisted, waving a spatula in her direction.

A spot of butter flicked onto her glasses. She whipped them off. He reached for a towel and took them from her hands.

"Why, Ms. Stickert, you're beautiful without your glasses!"

"Right."

When the towel only smeared her lenses, he lifted

the hem of his untucked shirt to use, revealing a slash of sun-tanned abdomen. He was smooth as a well-made bed, Gwen thought with growing irritation as she glanced away.

Beds and Dave, fantasies and Dave . . . She had to stop this now!

Dave was a sweetheart. A lighthearted guy with no aims in life save illustrating comic books and tackling the odd advertising job. From what she'd heard, he did well in his field, if you could call it a field. Judging from the sporty red Camaro in the drive, he never lacked for contracts or creature comforts.

So he was successful. In his way. Which meant ambition never interfered with a good time. Neither did deadlines or budgets. A free spirit, his major passion lay in remaining that way—as far as she could tell. Even his drawing was more joy than job.

Oomph! Gwen thought, visualizing the comic book graphics just above her head. Nothing so aptly described Dave's unwitting effect on her.

At six foot two, he'd grown from lanky to lean. A spare tire would never settle on that waistline. The man ate for sinfully delicious pleasure. Nothing as mundane as calories clung to him.

And he kissed like a hot desert wind.

"Here you are." He handed over her glasses.

They helped her focus on him up close. His hair was at least four shades of blond, as if, unable to make up his mind, he'd let the sun decide. Finger-combed strands strayed across his forehead in careless rays, a ruffled, inviting tangle.

He had a perfect nose, rakishly crooked due to a surfing accident, and a face that, unlike hers, was lined only where it had to be. Wrinkles underlined eyes the color of copper pennies. A set of parentheses captured the cant of his smile, the curve of lips she'd tasted once. Tasted still.

"Hope you're hungry," he said.

More than he'd every know, she thought.

Caught up in the romance of the wedding reception, they'd flirted.

"Moondance" had been the song, and their dance had ended in a kiss, a dip. Dave could have lowered her all the way to the floor and she wouldn't have minded. She'd made that abundantly clear.

Poor Dave. Butter wouldn't melt in his mouth, although *she* almost had. She'd put her tongue— good Lord! He probably thought her depraved. Just because certain of her needs had gone unmet for too long, was no excuse for inflicting them on him.

True then, true now.

But another thought tormented her. Maybe his good-natured teasing was his way of drawing the line, acknowledging the desire she all too blatantly displayed while never following up on it. He probably pitied her.

Gwen, you're being as melodramatic as Charlotte! a tiny voice inside her insisted.

Too late. The very thought robbed her of all appetite. Whatever Dave was cooking up would have to wait. Once Charlotte and Robert were safely back to hammer and tongs instead of nuclear warheads, she'd flee.

"Looks like we've got ourselves roped into some peacemaking," she said, forcing cheeriness into her voice. "I studied accounting, not political science."

"Bet that isn't what you told Charlotte."

"Actually, I could've turned Charlotte down. You don't grow up with these theatrics without learning a little self-defense. It was mother I couldn't say no to. At least I get some time to study. What do you get out of this?"

"Gram promised to leave me her bingo winnings. A sizable fortune, I assure you. Plus, I hoped the antagonists might give me ideas for my *Conquistadors of the Cosmos* series. Bloodshed, butchery, carnage, slaughter, the entire comic book spectrum."

"Do you ever stop kidding?"

"Often." He looked right at her, letting the eggs

sizzle in the pan. "Uh-oh. Take cover. Here come the combatants now." He snaked an arm around her waist and gallantly drew her behind him. "I shall defend thee to the death, Lady Gweneth. From fire-breathing witches and evil-minded magicians."

Gwen's heart turned over and a wistful sigh escaped her. If only they weren't so far apart in age, ambition, height, looks, sex appeal. You name it, they didn't have it in common. All they really shared was Charlotte and Robert.

"Life's a beach, indeed," Gwen murmured.

Dave's answering chuckle sent shivers down her spine.

"You never let anything go. Never consider my point of view," Charlotte went on.

Robert treaded calmly through the dining room. "I don't think I could so much as imagine your point of view, Charlotte. The skewed ravings of an hysteric are out of my range."

"You beast!"

"Temper, temper. Shrieking frightens the wildlife."

"Charlotte!" Gwen grabbed her sister's arm, deftly removing the pewter plate before it went flying. She tugged Charlotte around the oval oak table in the dining area. "Come over here and help me set places for dinner."

"Rob, you want to grab some more eggs for me?" Dave asked.

At his brother's behest, Robert grudgingly withdrew to the far end of the kitchen. "At least I won't hurl them."

"Was that what that was on the wall?" Dave asked curiously.

"Last night's property settlement discussion."

"Took me ten minutes to scrape it off," Dave added.

Robert raised his voice slightly. "Some things are more difficult to remove than others. Spouses, for instance."

"I heard that!"

"You were meant to."

"You swine!"

"Better a swine than a bi—"

"Biscuits anyone?" Dave announced quickly.

"I'd love some," Gwen replied, thanking him with a glance. "Make those buttermilk ones you made last Christmas morning."

"I thought they made your mouth stick shut—ah, another good idea. One batch of buttermilks, coming up."

He lowered his voice as she lifted a bottle of grape juice from the refrigerator. "I think we're going to work very well together. Partner."

Nothing short of sticking her head in the freezer would cool her reaction to that voice. Her cheeks flamed. Regaining control of her libido, Gwen took it upon herself to hand Dave ingredients. It was too easy imagining what Charlotte would do if she got her hands on a canister of flour.

"I thought I spotted some black rice in that cupboard," he mentioned.

The ingenuity of California cuisine never failed to intrigue her. Maybe Dave's cooking was as imaginative as his art. "None for me, thanks."

As she set the table, Charlotte clutched her arm, whispering urgently. "So Mom sent you!"

Gwen dutifully sipped her grape juice, feeling the enamel on her teeth turning permanently purple. "To keep things from getting out of hand."

"Me for instance?"

"The both of you. I don't know what you bring out in each other, but the Defense Department would pay handsomely for it."

"So what is Dave doing here?"

"Another member of the United Nations Peacekeeping Force, I assume."

"Wrong. Robert called him. They want to outnumber me. It's my cottage and I'm keeping it."

"You put it in both names."

"I was blinded by love."

"A good reason not to fall in the first place."

Charlotte swiped Gwen's *Statistical Applications* textbook off the table. "You keep your nose in this and you'll never have to worry, will you?"

Gwen quelled her with a level gaze. For some reason, she had very little patience with the two of them. Due to lack of sleep maybe, or disgust at love gone sour. They'd been so happy once. For about ten minutes in the late eighties.

Voice catching, Charlotte resorted to her best beseeching look. "I can't fight two of them, Gwen. It isn't fair."

True, Gwen thought, feeling a tad guilty and a whole lot manipulated. "I'm not getting in the middle of any fights," she insisted firmly. "The only underhanded thing about Dave is the way he flips omelets."

"If you say so," Charlotte replied contritely.

"Honestly, he doesn't even turn my head." Although the kiss he'd planted on her neck, a friendly family kiss, had nearly turned her knees to jelly. "I promise no one's ganging up on you."

Charlotte kissed the air on either side of Gwen's head. "You're a lifesaver!"

If she had to be a candy, a sucker came more readily to mind.

"Dinner's on," Dave called. "Time to eat or be eaten."

Dreading an hour of insults and accusations, Gwen needn't have worried. She finished dinner convinced a more deliberately silent meal had never been served.

Charlotte fled the room as soon as she finished her food. His own exit foiled, Robert muttered something unintelligible and excused himself to the lower level. Gwen cleared the plates then collapsed in her chair. "This is more exhausting than babysitting two-year-olds!"

Dave grinned. "Guess my biscuits worked."

She laughed, truly unwinding for the first time that day. "Thanks, Dave."

"For what?" he asked innocently.

For being you. For being here. "For having a sense of humor about all this."

"Anytime."

Gwen lifted a decorative napkin out of the holder to wipe her glasses. She had more imagination than she gave herself credit for, considering the half a dozen meanings she read into that one word.

She swiveled her chair to peer out the window at the treetops groaning and swaying. Fog softened the evening light, as thick and enveloping as freshly washed linen.

Dave took a place next to the window, arms crossed. "Pretty up here," he said, looking the wrong way if he wanted a nice view.

The hairs on the back of her neck raised. Tiny ripples of sensation chased up her arms and down inside her shirt. She flipped up the collar, sweeping her hair over it.

A nondescript, overwashed sweater clung to her shoulders and hips and sagged everywhere in between. No one had warned her Dave would be there.

"Mind if I open this?" he asked.

She wondered if he referred to the window or the conversation, and nodded quickly.

He cranked out a window onto the deck. "We could go outside."

"I'm fine here."

He settled back against the sill. "Alone again," he murmured.

He was young, she reminded herself, testing his wings, playing out his lines. But deep down, she knew it wasn't true. He'd left that gangly college grad behind a long time ago. A man waited on her reply.

Confronting the undercurrents that bubbled between them might be a good idea. It was one sure, swift way to curtail her unrealistic fantasies. Part of her knew she'd miss them.

Another part said, *Get real.*

Dropping her wadded napkin on the table like a

gauntlet, she stood. Shoving up her sleeves, she walked over to the windowsill and boldly leaned her elbow on it. Hoping that looked slinky and confident yet dignified and calm, she smiled up at him.

It was a long way up. Judging from the hollowness in her lungs, it had been a long walk.

A cleansing lungful of misty pine-scented air caught in her throat when he ran his fingers down her bared arm. That didn't have to be a come-on, she thought. He touched her all the time. Dave was a physically giving person. She owed it to him to stop misinterpreting it as interest.

So why did she feel as coiled as a Slinky at the top of a steep staircase?

"Kind of chilly in here," she quipped, covering up a shiver.

He unconsciously flexed the muscle in his own arm. "Maybe I should put on a sweater." He pinched a fold of hers between his fingers and gave it a tug.

Gwen swallowed behind her smile and inched closer. She had options. She just couldn't remember what they were. Any minute now he'd break out in a beaming grin and they'd laugh at how totally wrong they were for each other.

But things never happened quite the way one wanted them to.

He stood his ground, ready, able, and apparently more than willing to take things further. Drat having an outrageous sister! Thanks to Charlotte, Gwen knew all the moves but lacked the guts to follow through. "Maybe we should talk about combining our forces."

His laugh was as light as his hand was heavy when he rested it on her shoulder. "I thought that's what we *were* talking about." His fingers trespassed beyond the upraised collar, strumming the side of her neck tenderly, familiarly, just a hint suggestively. "You name it, we'll do it."

She could neither name it nor picture it without blood rushing to her cheeks—away from the brain that desperately needed it. She wanted *him* and would simply die if he ever guessed.

Poor Dave. He'd grown from lovable kid brother to intriguing man, and she'd never stopped wanting him for all the wrong reasons. She held her hand to his cheek and gave him a reassuring smile designed to deflect as much of her inner turmoil as possible.

The minute she touched him, she thought about sex again. In the privacy of her apartment, that was one thing. But there—

Women did and should enjoy sex, she thought furiously. Fantasizing, exploring, indulging. But within certain limits. Committed, verified, preferably married limits. Devilishly handsome, legally-linked male relatives who made one's heart palpitate and one's skin sing, were not people whose bones one jumped. Not in her value system.

What she felt was lust, impure and not the least simple, and she should be heartily ashamed of herself.

Heaven forbid Dave should ever suspect he had a sex fiend for a sister-in-law.

"You think Robert appreciates what Charlotte gave him in this place?" She indicated the trees, the view, the rapidly falling darkness.

"I don't know what Rob thinks anymore. Look at the trees. They disappear as if a magician folded them in his cape."

"Like Merlin in your *Camelot* series."

"You noticed." He ran a finger down her cheek. "You look tired," he said, surprised at the feeling of protectiveness that aroused.

"So everyone says. Tired and old, huh?"

He shook that off, unwilling to even consider it, and felt a tiny tremor run through her, as if a reliable line of defense had been casually breached. "You give more to your work than it can ever give back. Who gives to you, Gwen?"

She didn't answer.

"We could have fun."

"Why are people always trying to lighten me up?"

"They care about you."

"Do I look like I need a lift?" she asked lightly.

How about a life, he thought. "We're five thousand feet up, is that lift enough? We could move right in, live in the sky."

"Awfully romantic idea for someone who lives above a garage."

Thunk—the sound of Gwen bringing them back to earth.

"You always bring that up," he observed.

"A garage is a strange place to live."

Hoisting a hip onto the windowsill, Dave dangled one foot, fingers loosely twined between his thighs. She wanted to lay a hand on one of those thighs, to lightly squeeze the ridge of muscle. He knew it as surely as he read the danger signal in her eyes.

His smile enticed and warned at once, daring her to make the next move. *Take a chance, Gwen. On me.* Her picture of him was way out of date; he had his practical side. But Gwen had too much of practical. So he played the clown, showed her the fun she was missing.

And she chuckled and brushed him off.

Maybe he'd do better if he spoke her language. "I get a Malibu address for a fraction of the going rate. An accountant should appreciate the bargain."

"I didn't think fancy addresses impressed you. Or bargains."

"Only babes on the beach?"

"I'm not really that judgmental."

"No list of debits and credits in your little black book?"

"No little black book."

He stashed that information away. "No liabilities next to my name? No assets? No accounting for taste?"

She laughed. A joking Dave she could deal with.

"Still engrossed in the fascinating world of certified

public accounting." He hefted one of her textbooks and let it drop on the pile.

"Certified or certifiable, whichever comes first. I've been working all day and cramming all night for weeks."

"Which only proves my theory." He took her hands lightly in his, turning them over palms up, pinning them in place with no more than the pressure of his thumbs. "If you studied less and enjoyed yourself more, you'd be amazed how things fall into place."

"Your philosophy of life."

"Gotta have fun."

"Two months' rent in the bank and no idea where the next assignment is coming from, can't be fun."

"The money came through."

"And if it hadn't?"

He shrugged, his shoulders easily wider than the window. The outrageous parrots and gaudy cockatiels fluttered across the black and green jungle on his chest. The man himself radiated warmth, as if he'd just come in from the sun. Charlotte would call it an aura. Gwen called it the Tabasco he'd used in the omelets.

So he knew how to raise her temperature without trying. She didn't know whether to be grateful or worried.

"Heroes are in short supply," he said.

Her thoughts exactly, but it was uncomfortable to hear them voiced. "Why do you say that?"

"As long as people need heroes, there'll be work on the action/adventure scene. I never worry about money."

"Oh. The optimism of youth."

"Exactly how young do you think I am? Don't answer that. Maybe if I grew a beard." He lifted her hand to his cheek, scraping her palm over the sandpapery stubble, before he let her go. "Think that'd make me distinguished?"

He'd never be stuffy enough for distinguished. Sexy was something else.

She fought the urge to rub her hand against her sweater. The nubby fabric teased the aching sensitivity of her skin. Crossing her arms, she buried her shaking hands in the bend of her elbows. "We should probably decide how we're going to play this with Charlotte and Robert."

"Work out a plan, you mean? Put it on a chart?"

"Scoff if you like, but in an emotionally charged situation that would be a sound method."

"Mmm."

She wished he wouldn't do that. His voice rumbled like ocean waves, reminding her of undertows—responsibly posted but dangerous nonetheless. The sort one ignored at one's peril. His laughter rasped like sand on a beach, an incoming tide dissolving footprints carefully laid in straight and narrow lines. "About Charlotte and Robert."

"I say we play it casual. No harm, no foul. Blow the whistle only if the game gets out of hand."

And if they got out of hand? Gwen thought. He hadn't specified, and she no longer had the nerve to ask.

To top it off, she was deathly afraid she'd lost her voice. Somewhere on her imaginary beach, no doubt. Some guy with a metal detector would probably find it buried there, right next to her common sense.

She shoved her glasses all the way to the bridge of her nose, batting her eyelashes against the lenses. "Charlotte won't give up the cottage."

"Am I supposed to relay that message?"

"This is between you and me."

"Just the way I like it. Okay then, for your information, Rob won't surrender either. Somebody ought to tell him lawyers who represent themselves have dupes for clients."

"I believe that's 'fools.'"

"Don't worry. Rob qualifies on both counts. Somewhere along the line he forgot a wife is not an opponent."

She silently awarded him a point for maturity, but

couldn't think of a way of voicing the compliment without sounding patronizing.

Darn it, it *was* patronizing! Why weren't there more great men in the world her age, single, unembittered by divorce or child support, with stomachs as flat and grins as wide? She'd thought once Charlotte had found one . . .

"Lose something?"

"My train of thought," she replied, then sighed. "They seemed so happy at the wedding."

"I liked the reception better." Dave's eyes darkened and his smile quirked at the corner.

Gwen picked up her stack of books, arranging them on the table like building blocks for a fortress. "I do have some homework." Wings of hair skimmed her cheeks as she bent over her book. She invoked the hallowed silence of a library, hoping he'd take the hint.

Instead he grabbed a beer from the fridge and straddled a chair opposite her. He sang the words to "Moondance" softly, and the memory came back as clear as the music.

She ignored him.

He studied the multicolor amber of her hair, thinking how hard it would be to capture with ink and paper. Only pastels could handle the shadings of her cheeks, watercolor washes her creamy skin with its faint blue veins and warm peachy patches.

"Do I have something on my chin?" she asked suddenly.

"Sorry. Thinking of work."

"I don't think I'd make a very convincing comic book heroine."

He agreed. Gwen was an entirely different kind of heroine. The kind a real man needed—strong and steady and maybe a tad earnest. A woman to add obligation to a life that had kited by with none for way too long. He'd played the game with so little at stake. Maybe it was time to make mistakes that counted. Take a real risk.

She'd had a couple of glasses of champagne that night at the reception. Short of spiking her grape juice, how could he lure that dancing spirit into the open again? There was a woman behind that controlled facade, one he'd had a crush on for four years. One he might even love, if she stopped making him feel so damn adolescent.

Her condescension aggravated him, her distance teased. Every now and then, he caught a glance that heated him from head to toe. Then she skated away, and it was another six months before he saw her again.

This time he had a week or two at least. He'd erase those smudges beneath her eyes, light up those smiles, kindle those fires. Once again she'd be the princess he'd first met dancing at her sister's ball.

"What is it now?" she asked, patiently marking a page with her finger.

She'd definitely think him overeager if he blurted all that out. He spread his legs wide and rested his chin on the back of the chair. "Think we can weather the storm and come out of this friends?"

"Family feuds are known for their messiness."

"Hate to lose you, Gwen."

Before she could come up with a flippant reply, and he knew she was trying, he thrust out his hand. "Let's make a deal."

Her hand was dry and small, nothing flirtatious about it. He held on as if his life depended on it. "Whatever happens, we stick together. The forces of good versus the forces of chaos."

She released a gust of breath as if she'd been holding it all night. "Agreed."

A clock chimed on the redwood mantle over the two-story stone fireplace.

"Maybe I should check on Charlotte."

He moved his chair so she could pass. "Sound the drums if you need help, *kemosabe*."

"Thanks."

His voice sounded rough in the silent house. "I think we should seal this deal with a kiss."

"You would." She laughed, scooting across the living room before he could uproot his feet from the deep pile carpet.

Three

Gwen jumped, barely stifling a scream as Charlotte pounced on her just inside the bedroom door. "He's seducing you!"

"Are you gluing stethoscopes to the wall again?"

"He was holding your hand."

"We were talking."

"About what?"

"Staying sane around you and Robert." At least, Gwen *thought* that was the deal. She'd scurried away from his offered kiss as quickly as if a snake had crossed her path—the biblical kind that tempted unwary women.

"What is he up to?" Charlotte demanded.

"Six foot two." Gwen drew a nightshirt out of her suitcase. Either she answered her sister honestly, or she'd be pestered half the night. "You were right about one thing, sis. He's not a kid anymore."

"You be careful, that's all I'm saying."

Gwen sighed. Careful was her middle name. Maybe reckless would make a nice change. *If* she didn't have a sister to save from a marriage gone sour, a CPA exam to study for, a career to pursue. Maybe if she hadn't decided years ago which men were her type and which men weren't, dealing with her feelings for

Dave would be easier. Sometimes she wished she was the type for a roll in the hay, a steamy, tawdry affair.

It was no use. Women in glasses and Garfield nightshirts didn't turn into vamps overnight. But sometimes, oh, how they dreamed. . . .

The scream was bloodcurdling to say the least.

Gwen leapt out of bed, her nightshirt hitched to her thighs. Throwing open the bedroom door, she raced across the living room to the blurry figures in the kitchen. Charlotte was on a chair, Robert shouting, the knife glinting wickedly in his hand.

From out of nowhere, Dave appeared. He stepped between her and Robert—this time the gallantry was no joke. Gwen wasn't sure if that pounding sound was his heart or hers. It had to be hers. Despite the rapid rise and fall of his chest, Dave's voice emerged even and low. "Rob, put it down."

"Don't be an ass. Char, get down here, now!"

"Robert, I said—"

Robert turned toward his brother, the knife flickering.

Gwen shrieked and sucked in her stomach.

"It was a mouse," Robert snapped. "A minute fur-bearing rodent, a matter of inches in size and ounces in weight, and my dear wife has to scream the house down."

"So what were you going to do with the knife?" Gwen asked, peeking out from behind Dave.

"How the hell should I know? I thought she was being murdered up here."

"I was working on a screenplay when it scurried across the counter and hid behind the canisters," Charlotte yelled. "Kill it, somebody! Kill it!"

"Charlotte, calm down." Acting calm for Charlotte's sake almost worked to slow Gwen's own tripping heart. Until Charlotte screamed again, pointing at Gwen's feet.

That was it. Gwen was on a chair too. "Where, where?"

"Under the couch. By the fireplace! In the wood-pile!"

"I'll look there, you keep the kitchen covered," Robert said, stalking off manfully, butcher knife at the ready.

Dave nodded, planting his feet and crossing his arms. "Let any mouse try to sneak by *me*." A sly smile dawned as he looked up at his sisters-in-law. "I've heard of putting women on pedestals, but this is—"

"Don't you dare say it," Gwen ordered, shaking a trembling finger at him. "They don't scare me if they don't get near me. But I'm not about to have one run over my bare toes."

"Your toes wouldn't be bare if you hadn't jumped clear out of these." His face carefully devoid of expression, Dave sank to one knee, lifting a Snoopy slipper toward her.

Gwen grudgingly proffered her foot and realized she'd clutched her glasses in her hand out of sheer habit. Slipping them on, Dave came ruthlessly into view.

His hair was shaggy and unkempt, as rumpled and inviting as a still-warm bed. No wonder she trembled. None of the fairy tales she'd ever read featured the prince stroking the back of Cinderella's ankle just so as he fitted the slipper. Delicious adult quivers darted up the back of her knees and beyond.

Dave stood, his face a few inches below hers. A sleepy crust matted his eyelashes at the corners. A bedroom gaze slanted his heavy lids. "If the shoe fits, you know what it means." He smiled.

"Princes dress like this?"

He wore no shirt. His chest was hard and smooth, sprinkled with dark curlicues of hair. She imagined them springing to life after a shower, or lying flat, as if he'd spent the night sleeping on his stomach.

She shook her head. Just because it was seven A.M.

was no excuse for her brain to still be in bed, much less in bed with Dave!

He glanced down at the one item of clothing he'd donned, a pair of running shorts. "I had to throw something on."

The chest was bad enough, she thought. Dave sleeping in Mother Nature's own was simply too much for her to digest at this hour. "Spare me."

"And this was my big chance to impress you."

"With your nearly naked bod?"

"With my courage and fortitude."

That gave her an idea. A decent one for a change. "You know, Char, Robert did come running when he thought you were being murdered. Don't you think that's a good sign?"

Engrossed in stuffing papers into her briefcase, Charlotte grunted. "Probably wanted a piece of the action. Help me clean this up before he sees it."

"Did I hear someone say clean?" Robert sauntered back from his inspection of the woodpile. "First time she's uttered that word in four years."

"Don't start," Gwen pleaded. She would have hopped down from her chair but Dave stood there. If his chest was solid as polished rock, the table was a hard place, with Gwen caught classically in between. "Excuse me," she said.

He did better than that. He lifted her down. Her toes curled as her slipper-shod foot landed on his. "Thank you."

"We haven't been this close since we danced."

"Don't you start, either," Gwen scolded, catching Charlotte's suspicious look. "Scoot." She squeezed past him, stepping into her other slipper and self-consciously tugging her nightshirt to mid-thigh.

"'Wake me when the century starts.'" Dave read aloud. A dyslexic couldn't have taken more time poring over each word splayed across her T-shirt.

"I'm a late riser," she explained unnecessarily.

"Me too," he said, as if they were soulmates of the first order. "Going back to bed?"

Why oh why did every word out of his mouth sound like an invitation? she wondered. "After this ruckus? I'm heading straight for the coffeemaker."

"Instant's in the cupboard. I'll get it."

"No!" Everyone jumped at Charlotte's cry. "It could be in there."

"*It*," Robert said with a smirk, "could be rabid and carrying bubonic plague."

"Don't you sneer at me. In a house this nice, one doesn't expect field mice!"

"We're in the mountains, sugarcup. There are bound to be animals."

"You'd be cool if Mount Saint Helens were erupting!"

"I think it is," he drawled, "in semihuman form."

"Lady Gweneth? A word, please." Dave steered Gwen into the kitchen while the bickering continued unabated.

She pressed her fingers to her temples. "Maybe someday I'll be immune to it, like the freeway noise outside my apartment."

"We may have trouble on our hands," Dave murmured importantly.

"You're telling me?"

"The only coffee left was on that top shelf. If a rabid mouse is guarding it, we may have to radio for an airlift. 'This is Mountain Aerie to Base 10-4, send up an emergency chopper of freeze-dried, please.'"

She laughed and sagged against him. No matter how edgy the atmosphere, he could always make her laugh.

"There is one other alternative," Dave said. "Promise me you won't scream."

"Now *that's* an interesting way to begin a statement."

"Look up there and tell me what you see." He hoisted her until her nose was even with the top shelf. "Well?"

Gwen would've gasped if his hands hadn't been holding her ribs. As it was, she wondered how long she could hold her breath. The sun was barely up, and he'd touched her how many times already? "Nothing up here but some flower vases and old serving dishes. And the coffee."

"Any black rice?"

"Not for breakfast!"

He chuckled and slowly slid her down his front. "Black rice-shaped pellets are evidence of mice."

Gwen smacked her forehead. "And I thought it was some new California dish."

"You never had mice before?"

"In my last apartment, the roaches would have eaten them for midnight snacks."

Snapping her briefcase shut, Charlotte issued an ultimatum from the dining room. "Get rid of them or else. I won't live in a house with mice."

"Then you'll give me the cottage?"

"Robert King, if I didn't know better, I'd swear you planted that mouse just to scare me away."

"Not a bad idea."

"You hear that? You're witnesses. David, I want you to throw out anything they might have touched."

"Find me a flashlight and some wood, and I'll block up their entrances," Dave said, taking it a step further. "However, I will require the services of an able assistant."

"I'd exterminate Mickey and Minnie for some peace and quiet," Gwen said. "Give me a cup of coffee, and I'll follow you anywhere."

The house was perched on the side of a steep hill; pylons supported the front half, while the back was dug safely into the earth. Rocky, dirty, and dusty, the slanting site contained chunks of churned-up quartz that littered the ground like diamonds.

"You'd think these'd be valuable," Gwen said, turning one over in her hand to catch the lavender glints of morning light.

Dave wriggled his way up the grade to the narrowest corner under the house. "Like El Dorado, the streets are paved with jewels. I told you this place was magical. Quartz crystals hold amazing powers."

"So Charlotte tells me."

Examining the beams with a flashlight, Dave inched his way further and further underneath. Soon Gwen was all the way under too, toolbox in tow. She glanced doubtfully at pipes and beams and sagging insulation overhead.

"Neat, huh?" he said.

"Amazing." Actually, it was. With childlike fascination, she pondered the sturdy world of houses from a whole new perspective. "Did you ever lie on your bed and hang your head over the side and picture what it would be like to walk on the ceiling? Stepping over the doors and around the light fixtures?"

Dave lifted his head, his stomach muscles flickering under his T-shirt, and said in all seriousness, "I still do."

Gwen bit back a smile.

"Don't believe me? Join me sometime."

If she ever found herself on a bed with Dave, she wouldn't be staring at light fixtures!

"At least it's peaceful out here," she said. Birds twittered, the trees creaked, and far away a truck downshifted as it lumbered up the mountain.

Dave lay back and continued to scan the floor for mouse holes. Gwen looked everywhere else—the beams, the wiring, the indentations where nails had been hammered into wood. It did no good. Her mind's eye saw nothing but Dave—long legs, tapering hips, and a few inches of bare abdomen.

She suddenly clearly remembered three moles on his shoulder blade, spotted while standing behind him that morning. She'd been trying to forget standing in front of him. *Think clean thoughts*, her conscience ordered. "That T-shirt's going to be a laundry nightmare if you keep grinding dirt into it."

"No other way to do it. I'll take a shower later."

Great. Dave naked in a stream of water. One more thing for her not to think about!

"This is probably where they're getting in. Hammer," he requested, stretching out a hand.

Happy to be useful, Gwen dragged over the toolbox, ducking as she went. "What if closing up the holes traps the mice inside the house?"

"Then they'll climb into our beds during the night and chew our toes off. Why do you think I took the top bunk?"

She pinched the big toe sticking out of his torn sneaker. "Don't be morbid."

"I mean it." He sat up to elaborate and smacked his forehead on a span of wood.

After a silent second, Gwen unsquinched her eyes and lowered her shoulders. "You okay?"

He lay flat, head lolling, arms splayed at his sides. One eye opened. "A kiss would make it better."

"Don't be a baby." She wriggled up next to him in the increasingly tight space. Propped on one elbow, her other shoulder almost touched the house. She prodded his forehead methodically. "No serious damage. Now show me where this hole is."

"All right, but if a frantic mother mouse leaps out and bites you, we may have to amputate."

"You have the loveliest imagination."

"You should have read my *Sewer Screams* series. It had everything. Agitated alligators flushed too close to nuclear treatment plants grew to half the size of underground tunnels. A dozen unsuspecting maintenance men trudged unknowingly to their doom."

"Remind me never to let you read me a bedtime story."

"I was looking forward to that."

"You've got work to do."

But there was no rule saying he couldn't talk and hammer at the same time. "There's this professional dog-walker, see, and he's got six Pekingese on leashes and they pass over this manhole and the next thing you know—"

"I don't want to know."

"But you should've seen the way I drew it."

"I'll take your word for it."

"I've invited you up to my place to see my drawings."

"You meant that? That's the oldest line in the book."

"Older can be better."

"Thanks for saying so, anyway."

"Wisdom, experience, fine aged wine."

"You're on very shaky ground here, fella."

"And one good tremor would bring this whole place down on top of us."

"Thanks for the warning."

California definitely had its drawbacks. Earthquakes, endless sunny days, men who looked like Dave . . .

He signaled for another board, blindly reaching with the hand farthest from her. By the time she got close enough to give him one, she was practically on top of him. "Reminds me of stuffing telephone booths," she said with a huff.

"They did that when you were in college?"

"When they weren't dancing the Charleston, yeah. At least there aren't any creatures under here."

"Just a couple snakes and the odd scorpion."

"That does it. I'm outta here."

"Don't go." Dave rolled to his side, his body suddenly aligned to hers.

She stopped short, her breasts so close to his chest, she couldn't breathe without touching him, couldn't move her legs to maneuver without tangling them in his.

"I'm not done patching up. Look." He shone the light into the darkest crevices, then switched it off. "No scorpions here."

That didn't mean it wasn't dangerous, she thought.

It took a moment for her eyes to adjust to the shadows again.

"Didn't you ever explore abandoned houses as a kid?" he asked softly.

"Sure. Charlotte would make up stories about the ghastly murders that happened there and scare me half to death. No wonder she grew up writing horror movies."

"What about boys?"

"What about them?"

"Any exploring with them?"

A tiny tingle of excitement quivered down Gwen's skin. The boys she remembered never caused such tremors. "Charlotte scared the boys too."

"She had me going this morning."

His breath was minty and warm on her face; she drew closer, seeking the scent of him. The dusty cool earth gave a little, conforming to her body. She wondered how it would shift if she lay back. "You didn't think Robert was really going to stab her, did you?"

Dave shook his head. "Not the Rob I know."

"It was very brave, you stepping in the way you did."

"Not really. I heard how he called her name when he thought she was in danger."

He made it sound as if Robert had done the most romantic thing in the world. Maybe he had. "Think there's still some feeling there?"

"I think there's something." He might have meant Charlotte and Robert, he might have meant them. His voice barely raised above a whisper. "Maybe they should kiss and make up."

"Maybe they should."

"And us?"

"Us?" She didn't know when she'd started repeating after him. Or when, along the years, she'd forgotten how good it felt talking to a man while lying side by side with him in the dark.

"We should kiss and make up too," Dave said.

"For what?"

"For the last time we kissed." His smile glimmered,

then faded, like a candle guttering in a night breeze. "You haven't forgotten, have you?"

How could she? "No."

"I never called you back."

"I didn't blame you. A little champagne, some dancing, it got away from us, that's all."

"It wasn't the champagne."

"It was."

"One way to find out," he dared softly.

She sensed it before she felt it, his face closing in, his mouth speaking, then breathing, a scant inch away, the brush of his lips.

Her eyes were closed. They shouldn't have. Closed was a sign of surrender, a way of saying *Take me, I trust you.*

Her mouth went dry. The seconds passed, the sound of their breathing exaggerated in the silence. Someone walked around on the floor above them. Something scurried in the bushes.

Startled, she looked over her shoulder. He reached around and brought her chin back.

"That didn't hurt, did it?"

It tingled. It sang. It hushed any objections a sane woman would have and beckoned the desires of a needy one. It said, *follow me, now is all we have.*

Another footfall overhead. She cleared her throat. "We have to keep at least one relationship on an even keel."

"Do we?" He slid another dry kiss over her lips.

She dampened them with a flick of her tongue. "Yes, we do."

"I turned you on like a lightbulb once. You're afraid to admit it."

She scoffed, but that didn't mean she could construct a coherent sentence. "A kiss. Four years ago."

"You're burning still." One touch, a hand sliding up under her shirt, and he'd know how right he was. He gave her another kiss instead, on her hair.

She moaned.

"Every time I see you, I want to be around you," he

said. He nipped at her chin. "But you run away. Like Cinderella at the ball."

"I wasn't myself that night."

"I liked her, whoever she was."

See? He was kidding again, she told herself.

Her body wasn't buying it. Her heart refused to settle down to any recognizable beat. Her lungs inhaled nothing but the scent of him and their close surroundings.

When he opened his mouth, he'd taste like mint and man and morning. She knew that as surely as if the taste peppered her tongue. When she parted her lips, it did.

"Brunch was a great idea, Dave," Gwen mused from behind her menu.

"Sarcasm doesn't become you."

"Mayhem does?"

The Eagle's Nest diner sat on the edge of a scenic turnout five thousand feet up in the mountains. The thinner air had no effect whatsoever on Robert and Charlotte; they'd been arguing lustily since the foursome had arrived.

Lust. Gwen shuddered at the word and wished somebody would turn the air-conditioning down. Both raised goose bumps on her skin. Despite a twinge at her selfishness, she was almost relieved at Charlotte and Robert's carping—it kept Dave from bringing up their encounter under the house. *Lust in the Dust* she'd taken to calling it.

In seconds, he'd rolled her to her back, pinned her, and tickled her until she'd begged for mercy.

"Stop it!"

"Say you believe in fun."

"Tickling," she insisted when she caught her breath, "is aggressive dominant behavior."

He growled low in his throat. "The way you say that is a turn-on all by itself."

She clamped her elbows to her sides. "They might hear us!"

"And do what? Spank us? That's too kinky even for me. And believe me," he whispered hotly in her ear, "I have an imagination."

She'd loosened her arms just enough to let his hands slip out. He got in one more tickle, laughing at her laughter, involuntary though it might be.

"David, I swear you're a perpetual adolescent."

"Them's fighting words, pardner." He'd almost kissed her nose, her cheek, almost skittered another kiss across her mouth, his lips never quite touching hers. A yearning had grown in her more maddening than the tickling. What was worse, he knew it. He'd played her like a harp.

"Think we should talk about it?" Dave's voice rasped from behind his upraised menu, snapping her back to the present.

"While the fighters have retired to their respective rest rooms?" Charlotte and Robert had stalked off minutes ago to opposite sides of the restaurant.

"I meant this morning. Us," Dave said.

Gwen's throat instantly consisted of sandpaper and wood glue. She lowered her menu just long enough to make a grab for a glass of water. Cold mountain water with lots of ice might soothe that flush between her breasts that fanned out at the very idea of how the two of them had felt, stretched out on the ground beside each other, the sweet coffee taste of his lips, the hot honey taste of hers.

Ice. She ground it between her teeth until her tongue went numb. "Things got away from us."

"Not the first time you've said that. Or reacted that way."

True enough. He'd kissed her, and she'd responded with everything she had, everything she longed for. Her only recourse seemed to be keeping her mouth firmly closed every time he was near. If there was a cooperative dentist on the mountain, she'd have it wired shut as soon as possible. Not only would it cut down on succumbing to his kisses, it would be a dandy excuse to beg off conversations like the one they were having. "No reminders, please."

"And no reenactments?"

Her menu slapped against the plastic tablecloth. "Dave. We have nothing in common," she said calmly.

"We're both late risers."

"That's it?"

"We enjoy the same things."

"Name one."

He grinned.

Gwen turned so many shades of pink she practically matched the waitresses' uniforms. "That's sex," she murmured. "Not even sex. Kissing."

The Eagle's Nest was hardly the place for such a discussion, yet Gwen loathed the idea of spending another night like the last one. Playing gin rummy in Charlotte's room while her sister composed an alphabetical list of Robert's faults was not her idea of a good time. *A is for Aggravating.* "Okay, so we like to kiss. It's hardly the basis for a relationship."

"We like to kiss each other. That's a start."

"You can't build a deep, long-term relationship on sex."

"How about a short, shallow one?"

"Very funny. I forgot your childhood spanned the permissive seventies."

"At least you put my childhood in the past tense."

"Casual sex is out."

He laid a hand over hers. "Who said anything about casual?"

Four

Her heart tripped. She studied the warped and bare floorboards, the scratched metal chairs. He couldn't possibly offer her more than a fling, she told herself.

The odd thing was, the longer she was around him, the more she liked him. He cared, or so it seemed whenever he asked her how it was going, touched her glancingly, tilting her chin to the light to cluck over the smudges under her eyes. "You overwork and undersleep," he'd said.

She hadn't told him the latter was all his fault lately.

Making her restless and aware, anxious and wanting, seemed to be the man's major faults. Hers were too numerous to mention—lust, desire, limp spaghetti for backbone whenever he gave her a friendly hug that left her knees shaking. It was difficult keeping his best interests at heart when her body pleaded for its own satisfaction.

"If sex isn't a place to start, tell me where," he demanded softly, making her focus on him once again. Copper-color eyes held hers for a long moment, then lingered over her lips the way his tongue had, persuasively begging entry she couldn't deny.

"Don't get mature on me either, it throws me off balance."

His eyes flashed. "You're not giving me much of a chance."

She bowed her head, hair whispering against her cheeks. "We've got a marriage coming apart at the seams right in front of us. I have an exam. Dave, I don't need more complications."

Dave pursed his lips and deliberately relaxed his grip on the sticky menu. No, Gwen didn't need more pressure. He'd known that the minute he'd seen her tired smile. Any man could give her sex, passion. She needed lightness, good times.

How ironic. When most of the women he knew looked for fun with a man, Gwen rejected the whole concept.

He had one thing going for him: He hadn't been wrong about that first kiss *or* the second. His Sleeping Beauty, stretched on a bier of soil, had thrown her arms around his neck and shown him what a few hundred years without companionship would do to a fairy princess.

Enter the wicked witch, ruining a promising train of thought.

As Charlotte's stiletto heels snapped across the floor, every head in the place swiveled to inspect the leopard tights she wore, the irate sway of buckskin fringe on her jacket. The only thing missing was a riding crop, Dave thought. The haughty tilt of her head made other props unnecessary.

Disregarding the open stares, Charlotte reserved her performance for Robert alone, who was just now exiting the men's room.

Their paths intersected between two tables on the main aisle. Robert stood back, sweeping a gentlemanly bow so his wife could pass. "Ladies first."

Charlotte hesitated, then started to sashay through.

"If there are any present," Robert added, stepping into the aisle himself.

She almost tripped him with a spiked heel to the Achilles. He swung around. She glared. A stare-down commenced, trapping a waitress with a full tray. A true devotee of soap operas, she recognized marital drama when she saw it.

"And they're offff," Dave announced, grabbing the salt shaker to use as a microphone. "Vexation takes the lead while Exasperation closes on the first turn. This'll be neck and neck, folks, right to the wire!"

The audience of diners chuckled as Charlotte and Robert froze. Clamping their mouths shut was the only thing they'd done in unison all day.

Sullenly, they took their seats opposite each other with Dave and Gwen as human buffers. The married pair stared so fiercely at their menus, Gwen expected dark brown holes to appear on the other side of the laminated pages, smoke curling upward as the laser-like beams drilled through.

Gwen gasped to cover a laugh when Dave slipped her a napkin with that very scenario sketched out in classic comic-book fashion. Underneath, he'd lettered in title suggestions, in keeping with the eccentrically named omelet concoctions. Tijuana Tension. Szechuan Sizzle. Guacamole de guerre?

Gwen bit down a smile but failed to keep the answering twinkle out of her eyes. "Sarcasm doesn't become you," she whispered.

"I'll behave—"

Before her heart could return to its regular beat, his eyes darkened and he added one word for her benefit.

"—today."

Surveying the ladder to the loft, Gwen hoped Dave's promise applied to the evening as well.

She had the place and the players staked out. While Charlotte worked on a screenplay she refused to discuss, papers strewn all over the master bedroom, Robert's voice carried up from downstairs, arguing a case on the telephone with one of his law partners. Dave, meanwhile, had retreated to the loft. Radio blaring heavy metal, he sat behind his easel and worked steadily.

Curled on the living room sofa, Gwen closed her textbook with an exaggerated sigh and rubbed her eyes. Then she stealthily snuck a piece of paper out of her pile of notes and dawdled her way to the foot of the loft's ladder until the coast was clear.

She hastily unbuttoned the top two buttons of her blouse, thinking to slip the paper inside while she climbed. The image of withdrawing it in front of Dave turned her face too many colors.

Get up there, her conscience ordered. *It's not as if you're chasing him.*

Far from it. She had all the necessary paperwork right there in her hand. She settled on rolling it into a tube and carrying it between her lips. Warily ascending the rungs, she felt like a pirate holding a knife between her teeth, or a tango dancer biting a rose stem. Or a dog retrieving a bone.

To her immense relief, Dave overlooked that last possibility. "Hark, fair Juliet! I thought Romeo did all the climbing." Crouching at the top rung, he laughingly took the rolled paper from her lips, hauling her the rest of the way up.

"One crack about Lassie and I'm gone."

"You are a bonnie fair lass."

Charm. Why did he have to be so charming? she wondered.

She was standing so close to him, only the open railing by the ladder kept her from backing up as he glanced up and down her small frame. Her fingers strayed to her blouse, only to find the top buttons still undone.

The inquiring tilt of his head eloquently asked why.

"You're coming undone already," she muttered to herself.

She cleared her throat and stepped into the steepled space. A fan spun overhead. A box of artist's supplies sat on the floor. The radio announcer frantically declared a fire sale. A standing lamp, its shade removed, lit the easel in the harsh white light of a naked bulb.

Dave turned down the radio, waiting for her to say the first words.

They came out as disjointed as her emotions. "That's a good one. I mean Romeo. The Capulets and Montagues were feuding families too."

"It ended tragically," he reminded her, absentmindedly tapping the rolled paper against his open palm. Waiting. "Got a better suggestion?"

She came to him. He watched every careful step, his expression cautious, anticipating, willing her forward. The loft felt like a well-lighted stage, with Dave her audience of one.

A wry smile canted the corners of her mouth as she retrieved the paper without touching either of his hands.

He held on.

She tugged. "I think I've found the answer to our romantic tragedy right here," she said as she unfurled the paper.

" 'Our'?"

She handed back the paper and paced away, wringing her hands behind her back until she realized he could see the movement. She whirled on one heel. "Charlotte and Robert's. Look." She nodded to the paper, and he bent his head to read it. That gave her a few seconds to watch the light dance on his hair, to imagine running her clenched hands through that blond tangle, finger combing it, happily mussing it.

Dave looked up, his gaze capturing hers. For an electric moment it was as if he'd envisioned her thoughts and agreed. Then his smile broke like sun through clouds, and his laugh resounded through the loft.

Something in her withered. She could deal with anything but Dave's mockery. "What's so funny?"

He read her handout aloud. *"Fighting Fair?"*

"That's the title, yes."

"Sounds like something from the playground. And you accuse me of being childish."

Gwen stiffly pulled back her shoulders. "Twelve tips on how married couples can fight without having things get out of hand. It sounded eminently reasonable." She'd snapped at him, she could tell.

Dave pulled his mouth into a tight line and vigorously rubbed his chin as if deep in thought. That hidden smile made her blood boil.

"Well?" she asked sharply.

"Honey, being reasonable has never been their forte."

Her eyes flared. "I found it in a magazine Charlotte was throwing away, though I doubt she read it. Charlotte doesn't believe in self-improvement unless it involves past lives or getting in touch with your herbal tea leaves."

"And you propose?"

"We sit down with them. Point out how their incessant fighting is not only upsetting their families and their work, but tearing their marriage apart as well. Look."

She walked briskly to his side and, careful not to brush his arm with her shoulder, reached around to point out Rule Number Six. "Don't Hit Below the Belt. Now Robert is guilty of that, constantly turning everything she says into a sarcastic remark."

"And Number Eight, Stick to the Subject. When has Charlotte ever stayed on a subject long enough to work it out?"

"That's where Eleven comes in; Resolve It. We have to get them to define the issue, objectively cite the pros and cons, and come to a conclusion."

"So their fight will conclude."

"Exactly."

"Are you going to get snippish if I say I like the way your face lights up when you think you're right?"

Gwen's teeth clenched together. "I think snippish says it all. I'm sorry I came."

"I'm not," he answered in a rush, preventing her

from going. "Sit down. Have a drink." He extended his arm toward the futon, a lumpy mattress stored there for extra guests.

"No. Thank you."

"Nothing I can get you?"

A lungful of oxygen would be nice. Suddenly the loft was thick with stuffy air and unaccountable heat. He was so pleasant, and she'd been such a harridan. How was it she lost her cool every time she came in contact with him?

He touched her arm.

"I'm sorry if I was snippish. If. But you do your best to provoke me."

"I'm a provocative man."

I'll say! "When you laugh at me, uh, you push my buttons, as the psychologists would say." She pointed a finger at him. "No smart remarks either."

He bit back a couple, fighting a rakish grin.

Gwen ran a finger under her collar. Her hand slid down the deep lapels of her blouse, sinking to the opening where the hastily rebuttoned buttons barely held on in their holes. "Anyway. I should go."

"I'll get you something."

"No, really." Her voice drifted out on the last breathable air. "Nothing for me."

"You deserve more."

"Dave, I'm serious."

"That's your problem."

She felt the red rush to her cheeks. Hating it only made it worse. "I'm not here to talk about 'my problems,' whatever you think they are. I'm here for Charlotte and Rob."

"So I can stop congratulating myself on luring you to my bedroom."

"Your bedroom?" She glanced around. Yes, the futon had a couple of sheets tossed over it, but she hadn't thought— "You were sharing bunks with Rob."

"That lasted all of two nights."

"You like to be off by yourself."

"I'm not averse to company, when it's the right kind." This time *he* traced her collar, a lightly callused fingertip drawing a line down her skin. "You know me pretty well for someone who pretends to dislike me."

She denied it quickly. "I don't. We're just so different." She gripped his hand and removed it. "You're always teasing."

"Am I?"

She hoped to heaven he was. She cleared her throat. Again. "What would you call tickling?"

"Foreplay."

That did it. She was outta there. "I'm not into game playing, Dave."

"I want to make love to you. What do you say?"

"No!"

"Then what do I do?"

"Nothing! Dave, we're practically related."

"No way."

"I'm older than you."

"In calendar years."

"I'm wrinkled, I have four gray hairs—redheads lose pigment fast, you know—and in no time at all these freckles will be age spots. You mark my word."

He smiled, curling his hand around the finger she shook at him. "You need me, Gwen. I could make you happy."

"Sexually."

"Uh-huh. And in a number of other ways."

"Dave, look."

He knew that "look" and that "be sensible" tone of voice. Lecture dead ahead. He crossed his arms over his chest and rustled the paper between his fingers. "Yes, ma'am."

"I believe in sex as part of a mature relationship. A loving, committed one. It isn't Fun."

"With that attitude it might not be."

She stepped back as if he'd slapped her. He grit his teeth and muttered a curse. "I'm sorry, Gwen, I didn't mean it that way. You know how we kiss, how we fit—"

"Hush." Someone closed a door downstairs. "Just tell me what you think about the list."

Lists. Lectures. "Let me get this straight. You're going to sit down two high-strung heat-seeking adults and *talk* them into loving each other. Here. You got a better chance talking King Kong off the Empire State Building." He handed back the list.

"If you have to know, I thought one of us could sneak into town and make copies. One for her, one for him, one posted here at the cottage, one in Long Beach, and maybe one for each of their offices."

"Posted?"

"I never said they'd change overnight. They'll need all the reminders they can get."

Dave sank onto his drawing stool, held his head in his hands, and nearly choked on a laugh. "They'll find a way to inflict fatal paper cuts. They'll make airplanes and dive-bomb each other from the balcony. They'll cut them up and turn them into ransom notes and death threats. Oh, Gwen." He laughed helplessly, shaking his head. "Only you would think of reasoning a black widow out of eating her mate."

"You have a better idea?" she asked frostily. "And I'd appreciate it if you didn't laugh at me."

"I'm not laughing at you, I'm—" A guffaw burst from him. "I'm laughing at you, okay. But real life doesn't work this way."

"Wonderful. A man who makes his living from comic books is telling *me* about real life." She twisted the paper in both hands and headed for the ladder. "I should have known this would be too grown-up for you."

Now she'd pushed *his* button. Dave jumped to his feet. "Hold on a minute."

She held on tight to the top of the ladder. "I for one am not standing by laughing while my sister's marriage goes down the drain. Tell me when you get a better idea."

Before she could find the top rung with her foot, he'd strode across the room. With his back to the lamp, his eyes became a dark caramel brown as he towered over her.

"A better idea? I got a ton of them, Gwen. Most of them at night. All of them about you and me. I didn't realize I had to write them down."

"You don't have to be sarcastic," she muttered.

No, he didn't. But he had to find some way of reaching her. So far, not a one had worked.

"Good night," she said, stuffing the list into her shirt.

He could see straight down her blouse. Just what he needed—more visions. It'd be another long night, tossing, cursing, wondering what made an otherwise intelligent, good-looking guy a bumbling, fumbling fool when it came to one pert redhead who wouldn't give him the time of day.

But who'd gladly give him a lecture on how to build a watch.

"With diagrams," he muttered, picking up his pencil and attacking his drawing pad again.

"So sex is no basis for a relationship."

Gwen nearly choked on her asparagus. Why did he have to bring up the topic when they were eating?

Dave plopped down on the lawn chair beside her, resting a heel on the deck railing as the chicken cooked on the grill and charcoal smoke wafted into the mountain skies. The side dishes had cooked faster than the main course. Robert and Charlotte were inside placing blame right now. Dave and Gwen merely ate each item as it became ready.

"I said sex—"

"I heard you. Why not call Char and Rob out here, and we'll make this a panel discussion?" Gwen washed down her appetizer with a gulp of sparkling water.

Dave poked the chicken with a skewer. "Strong

attraction is the start of many a successful relationship."

"Opposites are notorious for attracting first, aggravating second, splitting up third. Look around you."

"Classic bad example." He dismissed her comment with a sweeping motion of his beer bottle.

"Constant friction leads to anger and resentment as often as passion."

"Do you get this out of a marriage manual? Never mind. Probably the flip side of your list. Anyhow, total security leads to a life of stagnation and boredom. If there's no challenge, there's no *life*." And didn't he know it. "So where's this leave us?"

"In your fantasies."

"Now there's an idea," he said, suddenly flopping onto his back on the hammock.

"Where?" She actually looked up as he gazed at the fluffy clouds. For all she knew, Dave got most of his ideas from cloud formations.

Hers, on the other hand, seemed to be generated in the pages of *Cosmo*, especially when he slung a leg over the edge of the woven hammock, the golden hairs on his thigh crinkling in the sun, toned muscles shaped by many a run on the beach. She imagined him in those shorts he'd worn earlier that morning, nothing else—

"I'll tell you mine if you'll tell me yours." He leered at her playfully, and her heart did a flip.

She thumbed her glasses up her nose and wished she had something to distract her besides a textbook and a shriveled chicken. She gnawed a thumbnail with renewed appetite.

"Would you hate it if I said you're cute when you do that?"

She mouthed the word "cute" and took a long swig of water, as if washing down the taste of it. "No one fantasizes about 'cute.'"

"Then let's talk reality. I think we'd be great in bed."

"So do I."

That's what nailbiting led to—it opened your mouth and words slipped out.

Dave stopped rocking the hammock and lowered his foot from the deck railing. His stomach muscles rippled as he sat up and rested his elbows on his knees, his hands gripping the moisture-dappled bottle until it squeaked. "Where does that leave us?"

"Right where we started." She sighed. "Babysitting Charlotte and Robert."

"When this is over, they'll be divorced. You'll be taking your tests, working your seventy-hour weeks. No more family get-togethers."

Gwen didn't know why the thought hurt so much. Heck, it shouldn't hurt at all. "See? We don't even have enough in common to start a relationship, how could we possibly sustain one?" She gave him a chance-ducking, apologetic smile. "That's the plain and simple truth, Dave."

He muttered a succinct opinion on truth and stood. Halfway to the door, he turned. With one hand he clasped the back of her head, his fingers tangling in her fine hair. With a none too gentle tug, he coaxed her to her feet, his mouth inches from hers.

The deck fell out from under her. Her bloodstream flowed thin as air, wispy as the clouds. The scrape of his hand moored her to the warped wooden planks beneath her curling toes. Fantasy fell away as he lifted her closer, his lips grazing hers.

"I don't want to hear it!" Robert thundered.

Charlotte's retort rang sharply from inside.

Dave eased off, promising himself he wouldn't forget the way her breath panted between her parted lips when he'd grabbed her, the way her pupils dilated, how she'd become speechless, stunned, acquiescent. He hadn't meant to go the he-man route, but she'd responded. Frustration was a valid emotion too.

"This is true, too, Gwen, what little we've got between us. We can build on it or we can run from it, but we can't pretend it isn't there. Not anymore."

Five

He turned and walked into the house, sliding the glass door between them, leaving Gwen gazing at her own reflection.

Grunting, she resettled herself in her chair. She sighed. She tucked a foot under her, felt the mesh of the chair making waffle-shaped indentations, and untucked it. She planted her elbows on the table and opened her textbook. Nothing helped. She kept glancing up at that woman in the window, the one who didn't take the risks her sister took. The one who lived her own fantasy about finding a suitably ambitious, reasonably sane, perfectly matched mate.

She supposed she could blame it on her parents. Everyone else did these days. After her parents' divorce her mother had needed the girls to be good. Charlotte's volatility made Gwen's organized common sense all the more vital.

Her reflection winced at the sound of raised voices inside, so reminiscent of her childhood. Who could blame her if she'd grown up believing emotion was a very shaky premise for marriage?

"What're you looking so glum about?" Charlotte asked, stomping onto the deck.

Startled, Gwen grabbed the skewer to look busy.

She prodded the chicken so hard, it nearly tumbled off the grill.

A moment of suffering silence ensued as Charlotte rolled her eyes beseechingly to the heavens, paced the boards, and generally gnashed her teeth.

"Want to talk about it?" Gwen asked.

"You think I'm miserable," she wailed accusingly.

"You can't be happy."

"What I mean is, you disapprove of me being so unhappy."

"Should I cheer?"

"You look at us with that frown you get, as if adults should know better than to make fools of themselves."

If the skewer hadn't been handy, Charlotte would have seen a guilty look all over Gwen's face. "I didn't know I was so transparent."

"You've always been the judgmental type. Not that I'm making a judgmental statement. You just decide about people, categorize them."

So she did. Maybe that's why it threw her off completely when people she thought she knew changed. Like Dave. He refused to be the carefree playboy she wanted him to be, the kind she could ignore. *We can't pretend it isn't there. Not anymore.*

Sweeping back her wild mane of black hair, Charlotte ruthlessly corralled it into a rubber band covered with bunched gold lamé. Using the glass slider as a mirror, she frowned into it. "I know he and his brother are in there plotting something."

"Char, really. If you'd been old enough to hear Mom and Dad, you wouldn't enjoy fighting so much."

"So I'm doing it wrong, am I?"

"There are constructive ways to express differences."

"And I should think them out like you do."

It was no secret Charlotte's passionate nature had always mystified Gwen. But Charlotte needed Gwen the Logical, Gwen the Sensible. She imagined the cartoon drawing Dave would make of that character.

"I'm sorry, I know you approach things differently than I do. But when you two fight, you say things you can't take back."

"But we've always fought. Only lately we bounce off each other like pinballs until you or Dave yell 'Tilt!'"

"Do you enjoy that?"

"I used to. Fighting makes making up more fun." She shrugged and hugged herself, adding wistfully, "We've just stopped making up, that's all."

Gwen listened to the trees creak, but hardly heard them. Ideas rippled through her mind like waves gathering force. Charlotte and Robert knew everything there was to know about arguing, it was making up they'd forgotten!

The implications raced through her mind. Slapping shut a textbook, she drained her glass of water. She had to talk to Dave. Privately.

But not so privately he's tempted to kiss you again, her conscience warned. Or the other way around.

"Isn't it a little late?" Gwen padded up the ladder to the loft. She'd gotten used to the dark on the way up; now she squinted into the cone of high-illumination light over Dave's easel.

"Inspiration strikes at the darnedest times," he muttered, a piece of chalk hanging from his lips like a beatnik's cigarette.

"Inspiration my foot. You've been at this since after dinner." She'd never imagined drawing comic books was such hard work. "Doesn't your back ache?"

He obliged her by sitting up straighter on the stool. Something in his spine creaked. Running a hand distractedly through his hair, he peered at the artwork through red-rimmed eyes. "Now that you mention it. Ever walk on a guy's back, Gwen? As the lithe Far Eastern maidens do in myth and legend?"

"Not to mention in massage parlors. Let me get a

pair of Charlotte's stiletto heels, and we'll try it, Quasimodo."

She cringed as he assumed his hunch again, his attention returning to his work. She circled around behind him. "Superstitious?"

"Go ahead, take a look." He waved at the pad, fingers stained by half a dozen shades of pastels.

Gwen gasped when she saw what he'd done, then rested a hand on his shoulder, instantly reassuring him. "I didn't mean it that way," she said. "It's just—"

"Awful?"

She nodded slowly. "In a way."

Dave turned and looked up at her, then back at his work.

She bent to whisper in his ear, scruffing his hair. "Awful meaning horrifying. I expected pastels to be gentle, subtle. If anything, this is too expertly drawn."

"You don't like the blood spurting out here." He pointed with a stub of red chalk.

"I suppose it's necessary. I mean, what with that sword hacking off the, uh—"

"The evil dwarf's mystical ring. Here it is still attached to the finger, down here."

Gwen swallowed. "Of course."

"Beli-Zar has to do that or the evil dwarf will reign over the land of the Amazon for another thousand years."

"That explains everything."

"You like her?"

Gwen studied Beli-Zar, the Amazon Woman Warrior. If Dave fantasized about women like her, she had nothing to worry about. Beli-Zar would be six foot eight in the real world. Pectorals developed to a solid 38D, her thighs would do a bicycle racer proud, not to mention the major-league biceps raising that glinting sword.

"She's got a lot of hair," Gwen murmured, tracing the almost living coils swirling about the woman's head.

"She doesn't look like anyone?"

Now that he mentioned it . . . Gwen glanced through the spindles of the balcony railing to the living room below. While Robert started a fire, Charlotte scribbled furiously over her new screenplay, hair spilling across the dining room table in a cloud of such inky blackness, Gwen was surprised it didn't have blue highlights in it, like the drawing. . . .

Her glance ricocheted back to the easel, and her hand flew to her mouth.

Dave spun on his stool, gripping her hand in his and touching her fingers to his lips. "Our secret," he said softly, a devilish gleam in his eyes.

A giggle rose in her throat. She wrestled it down as defiantly as Beli-Zar had conquered the dwarf. Grown women didn't giggle.

"We've been keeping a lot of secrets lately," she said.

"And creating a few." His lips brushed her knuckles as he spoke.

Her pulse thrummed like the dance music beat on the radio he worked beside. Her skin shimmered like the highlights in Beli-Zar's hair, the hammered brass plates that served as her protective armor. "That metal bra can't be very comfortable."

"Charlotte's avenging fury meets Madonna's body. Who says comic books don't reflect real life?"

Bodies. Her mind stalled on the word.

Until he spoke, she hadn't realized she'd resumed her place behind him and begun kneading his shoulders. He rolled his head back, eyelashes pale on his tanned cheeks, smile wide, shoulders wider under her working fingers.

"Don't stop. Feels good."

The man relaxed at the drop of a hat—a skill she envied. She probed her own senses for the knot of tension she'd been carrying with her for months, the one that loosened whenever he made her laugh, and loosened some more when he touched her.

"Speaking of real life," Gwen murmured. "I wanted to thank you for that race announcer gag at the restaurant."

"Humor can be very disarming."

True in more ways than one, she thought. "I've realized something about Charlotte and Robert that might apply to us."

"I'm not him and you're not her."

"Heavens, no. She's exhausting."

"And wild. But she's got the courage to let her emotions lead her—like Beli-Zar here. Fire and rage create an exaggerated kind of beauty."

A flash of envy pricked at Gwen. "And I suppose I'm a warm glass of milk before bed?"

Dave threw his head back and laughed. "Maybe I like milk before bed. Tuck me in tonight and find out."

She laughed at his open entreaty. "Sorry, sonny boy."

"Uh-uh," he replied. "Thought we dispensed with the kid's stuff."

Spinning slowly on the stool, he placed his hands on her waist and drew her onto his knee. Slowly they revolved until they faced the picture once more, shielded from the living room by the easel.

"I've grown up since we first met. It's about time you knew that."

She believed him. There was very little he had left to do to prove it.

Then he kissed her.

"No arguments," he said softly. "There've been enough arguments in this house." Openly, candidly, his mouth came down on hers. His tongue tasted coppery, metallic, sweet and tangy and elemental. As necessary, Gwen thought, as clear cold mineral water rushing down a mountainside.

She shifted on his legs, a rush of sensation sparkling under her thighs where the denim of her jeans absorbed the heat of his skin, the ragged edges of his cutoffs.

It grew cold and dark rapidly in the mountains. Caught up in his work, he'd lost all track of the temperature. It didn't matter, they were plenty hot now. His skin felt like a furnace as she rasped her cheek against it, almost purring at the delicious sensation.

She wound one arm around his shoulders, the other skimmed the side of his neck, her hand curling familiarly, femininely, up into hair fragrant with the dark scent of charcoal smoke.

He wasn't powerful, not like the knights and barbarians she'd seen in his work. Not even like Beli-Zar. He was lean, every inch sinewy and strong, so at odds with the caring, playful personality inside. He gave, he enticed, he never demanded. The man was too free a spirit to follow orders or make them. Instead he offered her all the time in the world to explore his mouth and the way their lips fit together. To take it as far as she dared.

She rested her forehead to his at last.

"Gwen," he breathed.

That was close, she thought. He already knew she loved his kisses. All they'd done was confirm it. Could he blame her? Lure her any closer to the edge?

When his hand closed on her waist, inside her silk T-shirt, she nearly jumped out of her skin.

"Dave, wait." She knew he would, even if the plea sounded husky and alluring in her own ears.

"Why deny yourself?"

"I'd be using you. It'd be physical and that's all."

"Have you ever tried that?"

"No." She thought he'd sneer.

He didn't.

"Have *you*?" she asked.

He shook his head. "Not lately."

He wanted more lately—a real, emotional, gut-level kind of relationship. The kind that got below the surface and hurt sometimes—like Charlotte and Robert's. Only he'd make sure he never let Gwen forget how sweet the achy, unsettled, early stages of love could be.

"We've got to talk."

"We were." He ran his hand over her skin, a thumb

outlining the underwire of her bra. She had a mole, a few inches below. He toyed with it suggestively, running his fingers across it as if it were a nipple.

The sheer idea made her blood race. Her breasts grew tender and sensitive, jealous at the diverted attention that should have been theirs. "I can't talk if you do that."

He didn't seem to be paying attention. Nuzzling her silk T-shirt, he bowed his head until his nose skimmed her collar, her collarbone, then the fine hair on the side of her neck.

Coming up the ladder, she'd had no more intention of kissing him than of flying. But somehow he seduced her into both by welcoming her, accepting anything *she* wanted to do.

Maybe he accepted the fact that older women made fools of themselves for younger men. Her skin flushed. The Dave she'd seen these last few days was the same impulsive, maddeningly unconcerned kid she'd always known, wasn't he? While Robert and Charlotte irritated her like nails scraping slate, he cruised through the day as smooth as cream on strawberries.

Then he'd kissed her until her knees had turned to grape jelly. She couldn't escape the teasing glint in his eye that said he knew exactly what he was doing.

But was he laughing at her or at them?

Gwen pressed herself away from his embrace.

"They can't see us," he protested.

"They can't see anything but their hurt. That's what I need to talk to you about."

Dave swiveled on his stool. With one swipe of his hand he ran a streak of pink and yellow chalk through his hair, then let it fall, untamed and colorful, across his forehead.

He was so endearing Gwen almost went back to him. She clung to her plan instead. "Charlotte said they've gotten so used to arguing, they've forgotten how to make up. That gave me an idea."

"Mmm," came the grunted reply. Head bowed, he dashed off a few strokes on a lap-size sketch pad he'd picked up, and handed it to Gwen. "So what's the big idea, Lady Gweneth?"

She frowned at the picture of a bespectacled woman with flying wings of light brown hair and a hundred-watt bulb over her head. Something twisted inside her as she tried to decide which he meant more, the affection or the caricature. He might very well be making fun of her, so why did her heart insist on glowing like the bulb? "No one ever drew me before."

"I'd like to draw you a lot of ways." He let the statement linger. "When we have more time. But you were saying?"

She was blushing. Firmly organized thoughts scattered like pigeons in a hayloft. She walked away, sitting on the edge of the futon.

Dave watched her hesitate first. He wondered if she smelled him on the sheets, if that made her hesitate before she sat—or if it drew her.

He wondered how she'd smell. Feminine, he supposed, honeyed and pale as only Gwen could be. Her hair would smell like perfumed shampoo, and lower, coiled and private, her hair would be reddish, maybe blond; he wasn't the least shy picturing it either way.

She caught him staring. He didn't mind.

"You look good on that," he said. "I'd like to draw you in this light." And in less. Lower the neckline on her shirt, raise the hem to reveal her downy waist, dispense with the jeans altogether.

She jumped up, as if visualizing the same, and swiped at the seat of her jeans. "Sorry. You didn't ask me to sit down."

"I didn't invite you to my bedroom either. Glad you came."

"Must be hot up here." She waved a hand at the peak of the wooden roof a few feet overhead. "Heat rises."

As if he didn't know.

Gwen nearly sighed. Somebody toss her a handbook of inane small talk! Blowing a huff of air at her bangs, she slid her glasses back up her nose.

"Heat's rising right now." He grinned and pointed to his cheek, leaving a chalky slash there.

He meant her blush. Why did he always turn conversations about Charlotte and Robert into conversations about them? They weren't even a couple. Never would be. Unless she made a total fool out of herself. Weren't desperate women supposed to drive men off? "If we could remind them of how much they once loved each other, they might remember how to alternate the fighting with the making up."

"And return to the status quo."

"If they stay married, the families stay together."

"And?"

"We might see each other."

"You mean date?"

She shrugged as nonchalantly as possible, tugging her T-shirt back up when it slithered invitingly off her shoulder. "Something normal. Lunch, movies."

"Something safe."

"I have been known to leave the convent from time to time, Dave."

He laughed. "You'd date me? In real life?"

She nodded, the movement of her head becoming more tentative as she watched his Cheshire grin growing.

"You've got yourself a deal. But there's a catch."

"Such as?"

She didn't mean to sound so suspicious, but he had that mischievous glint in his eye, the one that sent her heart tumbling like the skier on "Wide World of Sports," the agony of defeat.

"We've got a couple weeks to get through up here first," he said. "You going to study all that time?"

"I have to."

"Night and day?"

If only he wouldn't mention nights and touch her at the same time. He strummed a hand down her arm. "Date me here," he demanded.

"How?"

He scattered her bangs across her forehead, skimming her brows with his fingertips until her eyes fluttered shut. "Relax," he murmured in a voice any hypnotist would envy. "Enjoy the time we have. Muggy nights. Cold mornings. Long showers with me."

Her eyes flew open. She almost swayed into his arms. Any closer and they'd be pressed body to body, and she couldn't bear that. "No deal."

"You haven't heard me out. We reunite Rob and Charlotte, and you let me show you a good time. That's my deal. That's all."

A good time? Resting her head on his shoulder in the unrhythmic dance his sway had started, she fought disappointment. He hadn't been laughing at her at all. To Dave flirting was fun, Gwen was funny, and sex was probably a blast. Did he ever see beyond pleasure? To lifetimes and commitment? Responsibilities shared by two?

She'd probably have to peel him from the rafters if she even mentioned the word "responsibility." But desire spiraled through her all the same, slow and urgent as a coil of smoke deep in a forest. "Fun," she repeated. "Good times."

"Help you get through the hard ones." He touched her lower lip with his thumb, shaping a tired smile. It didn't hold. Plans spun through his mind like incantations in a wizard's cave.

The lady expected pressure. He'd seduce her with looseness, lure her with lazy days. Yes, she had her books and exams, but there were hours to fill, and hours to let slide by, side by side.

His smart lady had missed one obvious point. A reunited Rob and Charlotte would be living proof opposites worked. And Dave had never been one to avoid an "I told you so." By the time they'd dispensed with this marriage counseling business, he'd have her laughing and saying yes. Then she'd have to take him seriously.

"So what's your plan?" he asked.

The way her cheek brushed his T-shirt had his

nipples standing on end, his heart pumping. He was growing hard, and he didn't want to scare her. He stopped their dance. "Your plan?"

She blinked, took a minute to reorganize her thoughts, and spoke. "They've seen so much anger, they've forgotten joy. They need reminding."

He smiled, but kept it to himself. She'd be drawing them graphs next. Setting up plus and minus columns showing how the good balanced out the bad. "But can you *tell* someone that?" He stole a kiss. Cheeky devil.

"That's just it. Lecturing won't do it."

"What about show-and-tell?" Ducking a thumb under her chin, he placed a smacking kiss on her lips. "We'll demonstrate how nice it is to find someone you want to do this with." He insinuated himself closer, his body angling into hers, that chivalrous streak of his disintegrating as he tasted her mouth once more.

Gwen tried her best no-nonsense glare, *after* her eyes refocused and lost their dewy sheen.

"We'll do it all—" he said.

She tried not to gulp on the word "all."

"We'll kiss and cuddle and fill this place with the happiness they left somewhere back there on the road, alongside the slain and wounded." He waited until her mouth was dry and her lips all but parted, then planted a lip-smacker right in the middle of her forehead. "Good idea, huh?" He slapped her on the fanny.

"Hey! I never said I'd do all that."

"You dare disagree, Amazon maiden? Then prepare to do battle!" Grasping her around the waist, he twirled her until they flopped onto the futon. Writhing to his left, he grasped a pillow and thumped her on the rump.

She shrieked and swiped a spare pillow from under the covers. With a satisfying thud, it landed on his aggravating head. "Don't you dare tickle me again!"

"Boy Scout's honor. However."

She edged back on her elbows. "However what?"

"Nobody said anything about total war." He managed another swat on her well-endowed nether region.

"Wait, the feathers!" She gasped. "These are expensive pillows!"

"Bah!"

Before she knew it, they were tangled and laughing and breathless. Wafts of eiderdown filtered around them like her guilt at the extravagance. Laughter bubbled up inside her. She clamped a hand over her lips.

Dave tugged it away, and placed his mouth there instead. "Laugh with *me*, Gwen. Lie with me."

Part of her knew she ought to be on guard, the part fairly shouting that she was lying on a lumpy futon with a man she'd lusted after and run from for four years. Instead they cavorted, reclined, and she succumbed. Yes, succumbed. The word tasted delicious as his mouth claimed hers.

But she couldn't stop chuckling, clucking at the liberties he took. He slid his hands down her ribs, and she laughed again, gasping when he kissed the side of her neck, tensing *and* relaxing as his hands slid lower to her waist and tugged her down.

How far down she barely noticed until he stretched over her, the bed sighing as his weight pressed into hero. His leg pried hers apart, his chest flattened her breasts.

She wriggled, relishing the depths of sensation flowing from her breasts to her abdomen to those rushing tingles between her legs, so thickly denim-clad and so eager to be otherwise.

The laughter hadn't stopped, only subsided. She nipped his ear and laughed low like a siren. He growled in hers in return, laving it with his tongue, dipping, probing, breathing heavily on the sensitive damp.

Her heart nearly stopped, a chuckle dying in her

throat. "Do that again," she heard a woman's voice plead.

He obeyed. Instantly. Thoroughly.

Her heart hammered, counterpoint to his. No pretense at play remained. He may have been reed slim, but he pinned her effortlessly, tangled with her like the most tenacious vine, and pressed her down until she feared they'd both sink in the suffocating softness. "I can't breathe."

He reared back, hauling her with him, a large hand clamped under her head, molding her mouth to his, spearing her with his tongue. When he released her, her lungs expanded in a deep, needy breath—

Only to catch in mid-exhalation when his hand cupped her breast and he murmured, "Yes."

Their eyes met.

He'd lifted off her chest, but his hips still prodded the juncture of her thighs. The cloudy look in his eyes proclaimed his intent to stay right there.

Intensity. Passion. Things she'd glimpsed in him on rare occasions—when he was wrapped up in his work, studying a picture. She'd never expected that emotion turned toward her. She wasn't a woman to excite passion.

Or control it.

"Dave?" A tremulous question.

He didn't say a word. She looked scared. One delicate hand placed over his heart, and she'd know he felt the same. He wanted her, he ached for her. Searing desire flashed through him, a passion unsettlingly close to devotion.

Ruthlessly, he mastered it until the only vestige remaining was the rhythmic circular motion of his hips, pumping, borderline crude, undeniably erotic. "Gwen."

She swallowed. He watched the motion all the way down her swanlike neck. Her glasses were somewhere in the bed, her hair a disarray of silken cinnamon threads.

"Move with me," he commanded.

It wasn't the boy who'd been talking, it was the man who'd waited, who'd wished, who intended to see what kind of woman Gwen Stickert was—could be. He'd prove he had more to give than she'd ever given him credit for—four years and a fairy-tale kiss ago.

She closed her eyes tight, squeezing her thighs to either side of his, reaching for the sensations coursing through her.

She didn't learn that move in any fairy tale, he thought. That was pure instinct.

"Are you two all right up there?"

Dave bit back a curse at Charlotte's sharp, suspicious voice. A long-suffering sigh shuddered through him. He glanced down at Gwen, who looked mortified and doe eyed, and his mouth twisted in a wry grin. "Gee, you think it's your mom?"

Six

With very little grace, Gwen shoved him off and crawled to her feet, then staggered toward the balcony railing, straightening her clothes hastily. Tossing her head back and forth on the sheets had generated so much electricity, her fine hair could have lit a light bulb easily. She slicked it down.

What had he done to her clothes? No matter how she rearranged her T-shirt, it refused to hang right. Her jeans, tight and full around the abdomen, bunched around thighs that recently clutched his. She raced her fingertips up a surprisingly hot zipper as she peeked over the balcony rail. Surely she would have noticed if he'd undone that!

Arms folded, Charlotte stood directly below, a maternal glare fastened on her sister. Foot tapping, she waited for an answer.

Gwen waited for the question, but her memory wasn't what it used to be. "Hi," she said.

"I heard a scream."

Scream? The pillow fight. "I tripped and fell."

"On the bed," David called helpfully from behind her.

Charlotte scowled.

"Mom always said I could trip on my own shadow."

Charlotte's black-ringed eyes narrowed until no

white showed at all. "I was just about to come up there and make sure you were all right."

"You're not murdering your sister-in-law, are you?" Robert drawled to his brother.

Despite his sneer at Charlotte's concern, Gwen couldn't help noticing the couple stood nearly side by side at the foot of the ladder, both of them craning their necks as they looked up.

Risky as it was to stay, descending the ladder held all the appeal of jumping out of a lifeboat to the circling sharks.

From behind her a piece of paper tore with the sound of shredded nerves. Dave came out from behind his easel and handed her the Beli-Zar drawing. "Why don't you take this down and show Char and Rob what I've been doing up here?"

Gwen flashed him a look over her shoulder. "You behave."

That glimmer was back in his eyes, a heat-seeking, trouble-making grin. "New cover of *Amazon Women Warriors*," he called down, showing off his drawing to the gallery below.

"Riveting," Charlotte said, lifting both hands to her cheeks. "I think you've captured the essence of Amazonian womanhood."

"Glad somebody liked it," he said, bumping Gwen's hip with his. Unseen from below, he traced a hand down her spine.

Gwen clutched the railing until her knuckles turned white.

"Rob, what do you think?"

"Another man-eater," his brother offered, heading back to his *Wall Street Journal*. "Don't we have enough of those around here?"

Gwen had come up there to solve the fighting, not resume it. "I'm coming down," she announced hurriedly, stepping down the ladder.

By the time she'd lowered her toes to the first rung, Robert and Charlotte had rushed to the bottom, Dave hovering over her at the top.

"For Heaven's sake, I can do this—eek!" Her foot slipped.

Dave grabbed her wrist. "Steady as you go, there."

She inched down two more rungs, putting both feet firmly on each. "I took too many steps, that's all," she said gaily, disguising the tremor in her voice. Charlotte might be a mass of suspicious antennae, but it was Dave she didn't want hearing it. He'd know it had nothing to do with heights.

"There!" Safely reaching bottom, she slapped at her jeans, surreptitiously tugging on her T-shirt. It felt totally askew, like her self-image. A thirty-four-year-old woman pillow fighting like some teenager discovering sex-play! *Really, Gwen.*

Momentarily chastened, she ran a hand through her hair, hoping to pluck out any offending feathers.

Charlotte's beady look prevented her from neatening further. Sidling toward the dining room table with a come-hither look that would've intrigued a blind man, Charlotte discreetly cleared her throat.

"What is it?" Gwen asked briskly, heading for the kitchen and a glass of lemonade first. Under these bright lights, the red in her cheeks wouldn't fool Charlotte for long.

"There's something I want to show you. But not here."

Gwen gulped down the tangy drink while Charlotte locked her briefcase before heading out on the trek across the living room past Robert.

"What's the big secret?" Gwen asked when they were alone in the master bedroom.

"You tell me." Charlotte dumped the briefcase on the bed and plopped down beside it.

"You going to glare at me all night?" Gwen dared, tilting her chin, bravado underlining her words. She stared right at her younger sister.

But Charlotte rarely lost when it came to these scenes. She rose, crossed the room in four dramatic strides, and lifted the edge of Gwen's T-shirt, running the material through her fingers. "Dry-clean only," she said as if that summed it up.

Gwen glanced down, then swung around and stared, speechless and horrified, at the dresser mirror. One big, male, red, yellow, and ocher handprint outlined the underside of her breast in shocking pastels.

At least it stopped her worrying about the color in her face—that had drained to a pasty white. "Uh . . ."

Charlotte needed no explanation. She'd jumped to her own conclusion. "I told you he was trying to seduce you."

"That wasn't it."

"Then let me guess. Finger-painting lessons?"

"We were talking about you. Robert too."

"Yes! Uh, no. Well, maybe so!" she concluded triumphantly. "Oh, were you? And Dave chose to demonstrate? With the neurotic, one expects this," Charlotte intoned primly, "but when the sane flip out, it's much more tragic, don't you think? I expected more of you, Gwen. More self-control."

"And what about you? Darn it, Charlotte, you and Robert were happily married once. Maybe if you did a little more"—she flicked at her shirt—"a little more finger painting, you'd stay married! You've forgotten to have fun."

"This from the expert on working your way to a life of singularity?"

"Don't get me off the subject. You've forgotten everything but how to insult each other. Somebody's got to give a little, to shrug off the snide remarks and not return them arrow for poisoned arrow."

"Cupid imagery. I could use that." Charlotte clicked open the tumblers on her briefcase and jotted a note. Finished, she looked up. "Dave's distracting you so Robert can steal my screenplay."

"Charlotte! Robert has no intention of becoming a screenwriter."

"No?" Charlotte withdrew the title page and handed

it over. "This baby's gonna make *War of the Roses* look like 'Mister Rogers' Neighborhood.'"

Gwen gasped. "You're writing a screenplay about your divorce?"

"I'm converting my pain into art," she stated. "It'll get me out of horror flicks."

"It'll ruin your marriage once and for all!"

"What's to save?"

Gwen lowered the sheet of paper and looked at her sister. She'd had but a taste of happiness in Dave's arms. For a handful of seconds, she'd known the sensation of forgetting there were any other people in the world. Of wanting no others. Of wanting one man so strongly, she'd risk the keenest kind of vulner- ability—and trust him to give in return.

It was earthshaking, life-changing.

But Charlotte couldn't wait to hammer a final nail in the coffin of her own love.

"Don't you want to save it?" Gwen asked. It sounded ingenuous, even naive. But Gwen wasn't surprised when tears sprang into Charlotte's eyes.

"He'd sneer if I asked him to. You've seen him sneer."

Gwen nodded sympathetically. "But someone has to make the first move. To bend."

"And let him win?"

Gwen sighed and handed back the title page. "Maybe you're right."

"You promised me you wouldn't take sides," Char- lotte said, wounded.

So she had. But Gwen wasn't giving up yet. The only hope she and Dave had was reuniting this pair. If their families split apart, it'd be too easy for them to do the same. He'd charmed her, but how soon would she revert to caution if no ties bound them?

The risks she'd taken fired her still. She wanted Dave kissing her again, daring her. She wanted the ineffable thrill of daring herself.

Dave hadn't laughed at her longings at all. Hadn't run at the idea of a relationship. Hadn't sneered.

A shiver coursed through her at the thought of what a cutting remark could do to a woman when she was vulnerable, and she felt deeply for her sister. But Dave had a point, lecturing these two wouldn't work. Maybe showing them happiness and compromise might do the trick.

When it had, she and Dave could follow their own burning path.

Dave filled in the last bright strokes of Beli-Zar's raised sword. Pastels weren't usually his medium. He'd chosen something new to get his creative juices flowing. Even if it meant reinking the final version at his studio, he was pleased. It was what he'd come to the mountains for. Light, color, action. To get life and fury back into his work.

He snorted. Stubby crayons hadn't been his inspiration. Gwen had. Her sanity amid the tension and anxiety in the house charmed him. She positively glowed with serenity and common sense.

He admired the way she mapped out her life and stuck to it. He respected her self-control, her determination, even her fears. He loved the way she came unhinged in his arms; dependable, sensible Gwen unraveling.

She responded whenever he whispered her name, touched her skin. But sex was only an opening, a way to reach her.

There was passion in that little package. A woman every bit as fiery as Beli-Zar, but softer, gentler, capable of being his.

And yet, she defended her vulnerability with all the barricades the Amazon women erected around their fortress of Sanda-Thusela.

Dave drew the ridge of a far-off castle on a jungle mountaintop in the background, then stood back to spray fixative on the pastel to prevent smearing.

"Beli-Zar, would you take me seriously?" he asked softly. "Or would you cut me dead?"

Her D-cup brass cones reflected dully. Beli-Zar had no time for fun. She had a country to defend from conquering hordes. Lady Gweneth had less time to spare him, a week, maybe two. She'd laughed with him and lain with him and might have loved him given more time.

But would she consider a life with him?

Dave unsnapped the drawing from the easel and let it glide to a clean corner of the floor. Dousing the light, he stripped off his clothes. Twisting in the tangled sheets, inhaling her lingering scent, pricked by the occasionally quill tip of a loose feather, he knew all the swords, dwarfs, and potions in the world wouldn't help him win her. He had nothing but himself to offer.

Look how she laughs when you give her a chance, he thought. But his flesh heated at the memory of her laughter, her body quivering beneath his. A heavy pulsing throb reminded him how alone he was.

Did he give her what she needed and keep her laughing? Or did he take what *he* needed? The whole woman, faults and fears and desires.

"You want more than sex, buddy," he thought grimly. Kisses made this frog a prince in her eyes, but would she see him that way when the kissing stopped?

The morning fog had barely burned off the top layer of trees when Gwen rolled out of the hammock, stretched the kinks out of her back, and padded into the house. Robert and Charlotte stood nose to nose in the kitchen, fists unclenched for once. Unfortunately, Gwen and Dave were the subject of their conversation.

"Your brother is leading my sister on, and I won't have it!"

"If you think I'll back down on my reasonable demands because you dragged her into this—"

"She wasn't dragged," Gwen stated.

The couple whirled to face her. She turned to glance up at the balcony. "Morning, Dave."

"What's up, Doc?"

"Half the household. I think you might like to join us."

Before he could make a crack about joining her, she quelled him with a look.

"The happy couple," Charlotte crooned after Dave descended the ladder and joined Gwen under the dining room arch.

Robert's gaze slid slowly over them until Gwen felt approximately two inches high. "Sleep well?" he asked his brother acidly. "I won't ask where."

"You know darn well where I slept," Dave replied evenly.

Robert arched a brow. "And where did *you* spend the early hours, Gwen?"

"On the deck." For a second she felt like lifting one hand and placing the other on a Bible. She'd hate to meet Robert in court. "Ask Charlotte. She drove me out there." Too many accusations about Dave. "Tell him, Char."

"Sorry. It isn't my turn to cross examine."

Dave loped toward the coffeemaker.

Bristling at his careless attitude, Gwen strode after him, pulling down some mugs. "You coming to my defense here?" she whispered.

"Playing lovers was the idea, wasn't it?"

Maybe playing was all it had ever been, she thought with a pang. But the gulf between reality and the calculating looks coming their way was too great to bridge. "Okay," she announced, "this *was* all a game. We wanted to make you two see what you've been missing."

Robert straightened his bow tie with a satisfied tug. "See? She denies it herself. The only one crazy enough to think my brother is here to seduce your sister is you, Charlotte. You want her to audit my partnership's books."

"If you have nothing to hide, why won't you let me see them?"

"What are you hiding in that briefcase?"

"Don't change the subject."

"Answer the question."

"Shut your bloody traps!" The bland smile on Dave's sleepy face couldn't diffuse his bellowed command hovering in the air. "Sorry, kids, rough night. Coffee anyone? Gwen?"

"Decaf," she replied.

"If you think I'd serve these two caffeine, you'd better stop sleeping on the deck and start sleeping in the trees."

She almost laughed, then remembered their audience. Defiantly she turned toward her sister and her husband. "Look, you two, Mom and your grandmother asked us to help you out. We hoped you'd come to your senses. Don't you remember how it felt to be in love? Surely you can't forget that as if it were some, some dry-cleaning ticket you left in an old suit."

Wrong analogy. Charlotte jumped on it first. "You can keep your advice, Miss Dry-Clean Only. We'll handle our own affairs. You handle yours."

Robert pounced next—on Charlotte's statement. "So Gwen is here to start an affair with Dave."

"Don't be absurd," Charlotte snapped, "can you imagine—" The sentence caught in her throat like a hook in a fish's mouth and jerked her up short. "Gwen, I meant—"

Like saltwater taffy, the silence stretched forever. Robert glared triumphantly. Charlotte stood her ground, glowering at him as if her faux pas were all his fault. Except for one enigmatic glance, Dave said nothing.

A void opened in Gwen worthy of the cleft that made the Grand Canyon. At least she had the courage, when forced, to face the obvious. She was thirty-four. It was seven A.M. She wore no makeup, no beautiful lingerie, and had no coffee in her system. Purple crescents underlined her eyes, a Garfield nightshirt clung uninvitingly to her body, and flyaway hair drifted across her face.

She reassembled her last shreds of dignity. "I'm glad we're all agreed on one thing. I'm obviously not seduction material."

"That's not what I meant, sis."

"It's exactly what you meant," she replied, curling her fingers around her empty cup.

Dave put a hand on her shoulder. "Hey, don't you two fight."

"You stay out of this!" the sisters said in stereo.

"See? They stick together," Robert exclaimed.

"She's here to study, not audit you or seduce me," Dave insisted.

"Right. Like you're here to paint. If you were summoned separately, why'd you both stay?"

Dave rubbed his eyes, knowing Rob would slice him to pieces if his logic wasn't foolproof. "We stayed because some people would consider this a peaceful getaway. If you're so intent on turning homes back into houses, why didn't you two just stay in Long Beach?"

The couple's mouths opened for dual retorts and closed just as fast. They exchanged a quick look. Dave knew he was witnessing one of those moments of unspoken communication between married people, but he wasn't sure what the message was.

Charlotte hugged her briefcase to her chest and began backing toward the master bedroom. "I think I have some work to do."

Robert edged his way toward the lower level, deep in an unexpected thought. "I'm going to step downstairs. Shave. Shower. Maybe run into town and fax the office."

"Town. Right." Charlotte scurried into the bedroom, tossing excuses behind her. "I need to pick up another legal pad, an ink refill."

Gwen stared at the empty living room.

"Was it something I said?" Dave ran a hand over his chin.

"I doubt it. They're up to something."

"Maybe your lecture worked; they needed a talking to."

"Notice how they had to best each other even when it came to excuses to go into town?"

"Par for the course."

"Maybe. But I don't like it."

"Be calm, sahib, is nothing but jungle drums. Stay close to faithful guide."

Faithful? Gwen let his hand slip off her shoulder as she strode to the coffeepot. The aroma filled her aching lungs—or was it the heart squeezed in between that hurt?

"Don't tell me that bit about our sleeping together is going to put a damper on the entire morning," Dave said. "Look on the bright side, at least they came after us as a team."

"And we all agreed on something: my total lack of sex appeal."

Dave's smile faded. "I would've said otherwise, but I didn't want to fan their flames. Besides," he ran a lock of hair off her cheek with his finger, "I *am* setting out to seduce you."

"Don't."

"Don't what?"

"Pretend." The sting of tears startled her. She'd have hid them, but her glasses were on the end table in the bedroom, exactly where she'd left them when she'd given up studying the night before and had wandered restlessly onto the deck. Chapter 17, "Risk Management in Mutual Funds," had flooded her thoughts with visions of the risks Dave represented, the risks she'd take to have a man kiss her the way he had again. Foolhardy ones, clouded by wishful thinking.

Charlotte's relentless late-night questioning had

only put things in clearer focus. This morning was the capper. Gwen was all wrong for Dave. Anyone, wearing glasses or not, could see it.

"You've been playing at this game since we met, Dave. I appreciate it. It's cute. Even sweet of you." The firmness in her voice gave her the fortitude to look him in the eye. "But it got out of hand. We're here for them, and that's all we're here for. Let's keep it that way."

"Whoa. Come back here." He caught the inside of her elbow, her skin still cool from sleeping outside. "What happened to your agreeing to date me?"

"What happened to your tongue when Charlotte said I wasn't capable of seducing anybody?" She didn't snap at him, didn't raise her voice at all. The words carried their own weight.

"I agreed with her."

She stood utterly still.

Dave hated the way he'd hurt her, almost as much as he hated the way she accepted it as true. "Just because you aren't a seductress doesn't mean you aren't one hell of a sexy woman. Hell, you run from me every time I make a move. What femme fatale does that?"

Gwen shook her head, hair whispering in soft cascades. "I run because you're playing with me." *And because I love it.* She swallowed hard and wished she hadn't started the discussion.

"You open up to me like a flower to water."

"That desperate, huh?"

"Gwen."

"Dave, I'm only asking you to be honest with me. Maybe I'm a challenge for you, but we'll never have enough in common. Okay?"

He didn't have time to disagree. Charlotte came flying out of the bedroom, suitcase in hand. She stopped when she saw Dave and gestured her sister over to the door. A rapid, whispered exchange ensued, then Charlotte fled, a multicolor scarf trailing out the window of her car as she sped off down the driveway.

Dave came up beside Gwen on the side porch. "Somebody ought to tell her about Isadora Duncan. What happens if that thing gets caught in a tire?"

"Then Robert gets the house *and* the cottage."

Dave scowled, then laughed at her dry sarcasm. "She heading back to L.A.?"

"She asked me not to say."

"Are we taking sides now?" he asked cautiously.

Before she could answer, Robert came bounding out of the house, suit bag in hand, jerking his head to the side for a private conference with Dave.

After a couple of minutes, the sound of Robert's Porsche faded down the mountain and the bird song resumed.

"And may I ask what that was all about?"

Dave exhaled a long breath. "He's heading down to L.A. to save the Long Beach house. With both of them fighting over the cottage, no one's laid claim to the other one."

Gwen shook her head. "What I was afraid of. Are we supposed to police them down there too?"

"Nope. Robert made me promise to stick around so he can keep his claim on this place."

Gwen laughed a short laugh and looked up at him sheepishly. "Charlotte made me promise too."

A hawk circled overhead, its shadow momentarily darting across the drive.

Gwen rubbed her arms, suddenly chilled. "What happens to our alliance if the enemy decamps?"

"You mean what happens to us?"

He stood beside her, waiting for something she didn't know how to give. She felt the heat of his skin, the tickling hairs on his arm, a yearning she'd never experienced and couldn't quench. *Water to a flower,* he'd said, a choice between blossoming or wilting. If he touched her now, she wasn't sure which she'd choose.

"Well, *kemosabe*?" she asked, using one of his expressions.

Dave didn't return her smile; he made no smart remarks. Instead he stuck his hands in the back pockets of his cutoff jeans and ambled back toward the house.

"What happens is anything you want," he said flatly. "And nothing you don't." He stopped on the deck without turning around. "Want me to leave the door open?"

She prayed he meant more than the house. Trapped in her throat, her voice tangled with her anguished conscience. She croaked an "Okay," and he went inside.

She clenched her fists until her fingernails dug into her palms. He was her only friend for a hundred miles, and she'd accused him of toying with her, lying to her, even attempting to seduce her—just as Charlotte had said, but for shallower reasons.

She'd practically insisted his kisses meant nothing to her beyond physical reactions. That was a lie.

So was her promise to date him. She'd never believe he could really love her—not staid, predictable, boring Gwen whose life was set.

Apparently, no one in the house had believed it either.

Gwen took a deep breath of thin mountain air. They'd be there another week, alone, while Charlotte and Robert argued down on the coast. It would be better for all concerned if they set each other straight. Better, and more painful than she could have imagined.

Dave and Gwen tiptoed around each other for the rest of the day, as if testing the limits of the house—who got which rooms, at what hours. Only their departed siblings would be silly enough to make up a schedule, but that didn't stop Dave backing out of the dining room when Gwen studied there, retreating to his studio in the afternoon hours before dinner, turning down his radio without being asked when he glanced down to find her looking up.

As if that's all she wanted from him. She rubbed her neck and got back to her book.

They bumped into each other at dinnertime. Gwen hovered at the end of the counter.

"Want something?" he asked.

He'd promised her anything she wanted and nothing she didn't. "I thought I'd hand you stuff, as you need it."

"What I need— Never mind, I'll get it myself."

An angry Dave was new to her. It gave her a glimpse of the effort he put into the constant charm and humor he displayed when he was around her. He generated all that fun for her sake. "Ingrate" was the nicest name she called herself. "I'm sorry if I hurt your feelings."

"No prob. I've been going after something I can't have. Point taken."

"I was sent to stop the fighting, not start a new round with us."

"Robert and Charlotte's referee."

"And Mom and Dad's before that."

He gave her a thoughtful look. "Tell me about it."

The intimacy of his request made her glance away. "Not right now."

"When? When are you going to give me a chance?"

"Dave, please listen."

"I do. But I only know what I'm told."

"Meaning?"

"You say different when you're being kissed."

She grew very still. "Those are hormones talking."

"Do they ever lie?"

Her cheeks flushed, a traitorous declaration.

He backed her up against the counter, a flinty look of triumph in his eyes. The cutting board slid under her palms as she gripped the Formica and he pressed his body to hers.

"Who do I listen to? This woman?" He pressed his thumb to the frown lines between her brows, then traced it down her nose, across her swollen, tender lips, and hooked it under her chin.

"Or this woman?" His hand closed around her neck. His lips brushed slantwise across hers. "Who has the final say?"

Incoherence was no answer. A cracked moan helped her choke back his name. But an abbreviated gasp escaped as his tongue intruded, sliding over the enamel of her front teeth. Slick as tiles, slippery as good intentions.

He meant to kiss her hard, to punish her for what she stole from them both when she denied her feelings. To make her see the truth, to make her give, and give in.

She could tell him anything, but her body told the truth.

"I'm not a boy, Gwen. I mean all of this. Tell me you don't. Tell me you don't want to kiss me."

She couldn't. "We've seen what happens when opposites attract."

"Leave our families out of it."

"Our parents too? I listened to mine argue from the time I was eight until they separated when I was twelve. I swore I'd never be in that position."

He could have made a glib reply, but he'd made himself the same promise when his parents had split up. "We're the only ones here, babe. You and me. Unless you're planning on going too."

"I promised Charlotte—"

"You're staying for *her* sake? Why don't I believe that?" His mouth came down roughly on hers.

The phone rang like a shrill scream. Gwen fumbled the receiver from the wall phone and dropped it on the counter with a plastic crack. Dave fished it up by the cord and handed it to her.

"Mom!"

Stepping back to the taco fixings, Dave listened as

Gwen told her mother about Charlotte's dash for the coast. Fighting fire with fire, he added a splash of Tabasco to the simmering meat. One burning sensation in his mouth might as well replace another. Nothing could douse the burning below his belt. If he was lucky, it'd be nothing more than a dull throb by evening. If he didn't dream, it'd be gone in the morning. If he did—it would be another very long night.

Seven

Gwen glanced up from the hammock the next evening as Dave whispered the sliding screen shut behind him.

"Mind if I join you?" He dragged up a lawn chair, his long legs awkward as he balanced the plate on his knees. "Reading?"

"Taking a break from facts and figures. I figured you'd approve." She rolled the comic book in her hand. He'd picked up half a dozen on his trip into the little town of Blue Jay for groceries.

"Did you study all afternoon?"

"While you were gone." The hair on her neck prickled. It was as if every mountain watched and waited for some break in the stillness and tension surrounding them. "I'll get a plate."

Dave shook his head, licking off a thumb shiny from fried chicken. "I brought enough for two. Here."

He held out a piece of chicken, digging under his plate for a napkin. Gwen elbowed her way up, the mesh of the hammock sinking under her. She took the wing from his fingers. "Spicy."

He handed her a beer. His beer. She couldn't very well refuse to drink, any more than she could wipe the memory of his lips from the cool molded glass, or ignore the way dots of moisture smeared against her palm as she drank. "Thanks."

He took it back without a word, formed his mouth around the opening, and tipped his head so far back, the corded muscles of his neck stretched taut.

Gwen tore shreds of chicken wing apart with her teeth and tried not to think about it.

"You look like you're here for the long haul." Dave nodded to the pile of books at the foot of the deck, the end table with notepads and pens, the calculator, the pillow and quilt. "Promise me you'll come inside when it gets cool. Wouldn't want bears carting you off in the night."

"With Char gone, I think the master bedroom's safe again," she joked.

Her smiled faded the minute her gaze caught his, the moment she heard the soft challenging tone of his one-word reply.

"Yeah?"

"Sure." She nodded toward the plate balanced on his knees. "A power base from which to raid the refrigerator—which I'll be doing if a chicken wing is all I get for dinner."

"Have some asparagus." He lanced it with his fork and held it out.

She had two choices—eat it off the proffered utensil, or take the fork out of his curled fingers, which meant curling her own around them. She leaned forward and took a bite. He held the rest there until she chewed, swallowed, and took another.

This was impossible. Eating while Dave watched was like chewing tree bark. Her throat constricted, her tongue grew dry, and the beer perched just out of reach.

"Finger food," she chimed, tugging the last piece off the fork. She gnawed it as if it were beef jerky. "Dave, I'm sorry about the last couple of days, everything that's been going on between us."

"And everything that hasn't?" His smile flickered. "So am I."

"Compared to sleeping outdoors, bedrooms are some of the most dangerous rooms in the house. Did you know that?"

She looked at him dubiously. "It'd be easier if we avoided bedrooms altogether. Verbally and otherwise."

He dangled a stalk over the plate until a golden drop of butter fell from the tip. "Hammocks are dangerous too."

Didn't she know it. If she thought for a moment she could crawl out of this contraption without breaking her neck or falling flat on her patch pockets, she'd be long gone. "Especially for certified klutzes."

"I never said that."

He'd never said a lot of things.

Gwen made an ungainly attempt to swing a leg out. Her comic book slapped against the deck. Dave picked it up.

"One of mine. You like?"

"Yes. Really."

"I'm not fishing."

She reached for the book and nearly upended the hammock. At least her voice wasn't the only wobbly thing out there. "The hero was very convincing."

"*Ragnar, Viking Thane.* 'His physique chiseled like the glaciers of his land, his chilled bones and icy glaze terrify women and warriors alike And so he rampages through the Nordic world alone.'"

"Warm of heart and fiery of temper."

"Only to those who know him well."

Gwen flipped to the page with the picture of Ragnar by his campfire, the sky alight with fantastic slashes of color. "I don't know anyone else who'd paint a sky that way. So free, so audacious. Bizarre but somehow believable."

"The northern lights. They've got magic too. Eat." He handed her a chicken leg.

She sank her teeth in it, suddenly ravenous. "He reminds me of someone," she hinted.

Dave nodded. "He has great responsibilities, many heavy duties, but he longs for escape. A little like you."

"I thought of you. How his independence too often means loneliness. Sometimes, those who have nothing but escape long for responsibility."

He finished off the beer. "As Confucius would say, 'Damn straight.'"

She laughed. After two days of wariness, she noticed how deliberately he'd gone for the joke. Maybe she was treading on sensitive territory. "Do you? Want responsibility, that is?"

He shook his head firmly. "Too much of that going around. Like Asian flu. You, my lady, are a great example. Sit back."

He watched the way she daintily dropped the chicken bone on the plate, the way she rubbed the rim of the beer bottle with her thumb after he'd drunk from it.

"Rest," he commanded. "I'll feed you and keep you warm."

There were a hundred ways he could do that. Neither one of them acknowledged the possibilities. Instead he lifted the edge of the quilt, tucking it where goose bumps sprang up on her arm.

She snuggled in. He tossed the comic book on the stack of textbooks, then wiped her mouth with a napkin and crumpled it, banking it off the wastebasket.

Careless, she thought of him, but not about the things that mattered. She licked the last of the spicy chicken from her lips.

He rocked her, his hand on the corded edge of the hammock, tugging her to him before letting her swing away.

"You'll be singing me lullabies next." Eyes shut, her hand rested lightly on his. "This is so—"

"Shh. No need to justify falling asleep after a long day."

"Mmm." It would be nice, for a moment anyway, to

let him have the responsibility. She swayed as the sky blended purple and aqua, as startling in its way as one of Dave's drawings.

"They're very good," she murmured, "your illustrations."

"Thanks."

"Close-ups, pans, tracking shots. That whole page where Ragnar stalks down the castle corridor is one long tracking shot."

"How do you know all that stuff?"

"Movie jargon? I took a class. Two elective credits, I think."

Probably the one fun class she'd taken. "Eyes closed," he reminded her. "That's the rule."

Gwen obeyed rules.

When he bared her body and carried her to the bedroom, he'd remember that.

"I liked the part where—"

"No talking either."

"Why?" she asked, a touch rebellious.

"You don't have to pay me back with conversation. This is your night to be pampered."

Light and motion flickered across her face. A frown. Pursed lips begging to be kissed. She almost sniffed the air, as if weighing the pros and cons of surrendering to his care, to the lassitude he knew tugged at her.

Dave edged forward in his chair, dragging it carefully over the wooden planks. His knee bumped her hip where the hammock sagged, nudging her back and forth.

She inched away as if apologizing for even having hips, and began to speak.

He put his hand fully over her mouth, like a thief, and let it stay there, her exhalation feathering over his fingers. "No explanations, no sisters to rescue, no couples to recouple."

"Just me and you?" Her lips skittered under his palm.

"Tonight, just you."

With her eyes closed, it was difficult blocking the other sensations threading through her. The squeak of the metal ring anchoring the hammock to the railing. The sough of Dave's even breathing. Maybe not so even. When she tried to pattern hers after it, her heart sped up.

His thigh bumped her behind. She swung away from him, to him. *He loves me, he loves me not,* she thought with a dreamy smile.

She'd slept out there two nights earlier, after Charlotte had demanded once too often what Gwen could have been thinking, falling in bed with Dave King. Thinking? She'd been feeling. Even if their attraction was strictly physical, there was nothing strict about it. She felt treasured, sought after. The man made jokes just to hear her laugh, she knew that now. He prized her smile. And pursued his desires.

Her lips felt full, her tongue thick. A curious sensation hovered around her mouth. His hand was gone, but his thief-in-the-night touch remained, leaving her short of breath. She smelled his skin, smoky with barbecue and spice. Tangy, she imagined, wetting her lips. With a tip of her tongue, a nip of her teeth, she could have nibbled his palm, surprised him as starkly as the image had surprised her.

The idea quivered through her. She waited for the ripples to fade. What if he guessed at her fantasies? Would he laugh at the Viking raider he'd created, whose loneliness, whose need, took root so quickly in Gwen's heart?

Sleepily, she imagined being seized in one of Ragnar's raids, carried to his ship. A bracing wind off the North Sea would stir the collar of her blouse, the blunt fingers of a blunt man would undo the buttons—

She opened her eyes. Two pine trees cut through the deck, creaking overhead, looming in jagged shadow. Dave's face was in darkness, the sky a royal purple velvet behind him, scattered with stars like foam-flecked waves. "Dave."

He continued unbuttoning her blouse.

"What are you doing?"

"Nothing."

Ask a ridiculous question, get an unsatisfying answer. "That doesn't feel like nothing."

He smiled a private smile she almost didn't see. "Good."

"Dave—"

"Relax."

The hammock swung across a chasm of such spine-tingling peril, her skin prickled. Her nerve endings sang like taut wires. Dave talking and teasing relaxed her. Dave touching her did not.

Yet her body refused to spring to self-defense. The hushed clarity of her mind focused on every sensation with almost painful intensity. The hollows in her elbows grew so sensitive, one touch caused her arm to bend as if by reflex, her hand curling around the back of his biceps.

He let it. Then he opened her blouse.

Arching was no way to fight him off. The sensible part of her knew that. The rest didn't care. His lips ghosted down her neck and stopped just short of the rounded mound of her breast as he peeled away the lace of her bra.

"Dave, what exactly are you doing?"

"Enjoying you," he replied frankly.

Her hand slipped up his chest and lay over his heart. The beat was strong and steady. It didn't quail or tremble at the idea of what lay ahead, the way hers did.

"Kiss me," she asked urgently.

"No. Not yet."

She lay in the dark, trying to understand. She didn't know what he intended. When his mouth closed over her other breast, she cried out and gripped his shoulders. She kissed his ear, his neck, tried to run her hands down his waist, but the hammock tilted.

"Don't," he said, the hoarseness of his voice her only clue to his emotions. "Don't think, don't reciprocate, don't make me explain. Enjoy your body, that's all."

Easier said in the dark, she thought wryly, he couldn't see the freckles or sags.

"This goes only as far as you want it to."

"What if I want more?" Her heart sounded hollow in her own ears, her voice lower, as if everything from her vocal cords on down stretched, thickened, begging to be used in new ways.

He hadn't answered.

Perhaps she'd embarrassed them both. She clamped her eyes shut and felt the fire in her cheeks.

His fingers rested on the belt of her jeans, bouncing slightly on the pulse beside her navel. "I've wanted to do this for a long time."

"Just this?"

He heard the quaver in her voice. "I'd do more but—"

"You can—"

"I won't." He gripped her waist and kissed her abdomen, the ridge of her ribs, the sunken hollow of her navel. She was soft everywhere, her skin graced with peach fuzz of such delicacy, no painter could capture it.

But there were things in him that wanted to crush her against his body, against a bed, a floor, and declare her his. The part of him inflamed by challenge, by the heart-twisting knowledge that no man had ever done that for Gwen. No one had ever loved her enough to take her outside all her self-imposed boundaries. One of which seemed to be that sex was for lovers only.

Too late for him, he loved her with a yearning ache that filled him like a deep sustaining breath. But Gwen didn't have to know that. He didn't presume to think her a virgin, but he doubted she'd ever loved for the sake of loving, the sheer physical delight.

This was his gift to her. He wanted no sense of obligation clouding it—Gwen clung to obligations. He wanted her flying free.

His lips moved over skin he could only imagine in the dark—pale, faintly freckled, a band of lace and cotton and then . . .

She whimpered, gasped. "David, please."

He was on his knees beside the hammock, his arms on either side of her legs, his fingers uncoupling a belt buckle so hot, it startled him. "Tell me what you want."

More than she dared ask. She wanted ferocity and drive, the thrusting power of swords and the hypnotic, will-melting words of sorcerers. Instead he gave her gentle explorations and subdued, glancing kisses, light touches where she longed for caresses, nips where she wanted bites.

She wanted to be the woman to set him on fire. She'd never done that for any man. Responding the way former lovers expected, she'd reached shivery little climaxes that held all the thrill of dial tones. For a woman nearing her sexual peak, she'd barely used the equipment.

"What's wrong?" Dave asked. "Don't you like that?"

"It's wonderful."

"But?"

She dared. "More would be better."

She felt his answer in the tension across his shoulder blades as she reached for him, vining her arms around his neck. She kissed him, wanton and exposed.

He couldn't mistake her response. No man could.

She reveled in the crisp glide of his chest over hers, the give of her full breasts offered to his touch. She soared and sank on the hot gusts of wind feathering her skin from within, the rising power he unleashed in her setting her afire.

Her voice hoarse, rapid and pleading, told him where, when, how. The way she moved, the way she moaned, told him more. She'd give him anything he asked. And dare for herself, satiating the desires he aroused in her.

He urged his hand between her thighs, the denim coarse and unbearably thick. She wriggled to be free of it, showing him the place where she needed him to be.

He parted her jeans, burrowing beneath the scrap of lace. She was moist, slick. He found the core of her and felt her quicken. "Tell me you want me."

"I've wanted you for so long." She buried her head against his neck, then scraped her cheek along his, her face to the stars, her head thrown back. "Ever since that kiss. I've imagined your body and mine— Please."

He'd imagined it too. Which was why he wanted it to be perfect. Her body bucked against his hand. "You want me? All of me?"

"Yes, yes."

He slipped his hand free, felt her desire subside for a moment as she lay back, breaths quick and shallow, eyes limpid and welcoming.

She lifted her leg to his corded waist as he stretched over her.

"These cutoffs," he said in a raspy voice, fumbling with a buckle.

"Let me." She reached between their bodies and grated the zipper down, freeing him, teasing him, squeezing him in her soft, small hand.

For ten pounding seconds he was glad he'd kept one foot on the floor. "Let me take 'em off."

"But I need you now."

The hell with his clothes, with perfection, with plans. Gwen's breathy, reedy plea was all that counted. He stretched full length over her, and the world turned upside down.

She screamed.

They tumbled out of the hammock in a swinging twist and landed flat on the deck. The back of his head connected with a book binding. Her elbow dug into his ribs. When they stopped hurting, Dave laughed a long, rumbling chuckle.

Gwen said not a word.

"You okay?" She must've had the wind knocked out of her too.

"Fine," came her terse reply.

"Stay here." He wrapped her in his arms, bouncing her lightly as he laughed. She was on top. It felt good that way. He'd keep that in mind. The Gwen he'd just kissed, his fairy princess turned ravenous nymphet, would probably be amenable to creative positions. "Ow, hey! Watch your knee, hon. The moment might have got away from us, but the consequences remain."

Consequences. Acting on the truth about her lust for Dave, Gwen silently suffered the consequences. Rolling out of a hammock! Landing on the deck floor with all the grace of a roped calf! That's what she got for jumping his bones. *Just don't laugh at me*, she prayed.

"You staying?" he asked, a smile in his voice.

"You won't let me up."

"You're not exactly being held against your will."

"Then let go." She scrambled to an upright position, bumping him again with her knee. "Sorry."

He answered in a high-pitched voice. "Anytime, lady."

"Don't be funny."

He heard her scoot across the deck and assumed she'd found a place to press her back against the deck rails. If he didn't miss his guess, she'd have her legs drawn up, arms tight around them, blouse resolutely closed. "You got a better idea?"

"How about terminal humiliation followed by ritual suicide?"

"A little harsh. A lot messy. Did I ever show you my *Samurai* series? Tatsuya commits hara-kiri on a mountain promontory overlooking the sea. Very Japanese influence in the brushwork—a real change of pace. Didn't sell."

"David!"

"Yeah?"

"Stop trying to distract me. I was climbing all over you and succeeded in tumbling us both."

"What'd you think I had in mind?"

"Not enough."

Dave swallowed. Whew. Just when he thought she was shy and retiring, she came at him like the no-nonsense woman she was. "You don't believe in sugar-coating anything, do you? If I'm not good enough, say so," he said hotly.

"Please. I didn't mean to insult you."

"Then don't patronize me with apologies. Out with it." If it was possible to hear buttons pushed into buttonholes, he listened to four of them pop in place.

"Maybe I want more than you're willing to give," she stated.

"How do you know what I'm capable of?"

"You're so much younger."

"Just a kid out for a good time."

"No, I don't think that. Not anymore. You're a very attractive man."

"What's wrong with that? And don't give me any nonsense about your not being sexy. I think we proved otherwise."

"There's more to a relationship than sex."

"Some people get there, some people start there. You said yourself we'd be great in bed."

"But is that all it would be?" She waited for his answer. An owl hooted.

"I'm not one to make plans, Gwen. We'll live it as it comes." Could he say it any clearer? He wanted to live his life with her.

She didn't hear it that way. "I make plans. I believe in them. I don't think we'd work out, not in the long run."

"So you've perfected telling the future, or did Charlotte read your palm?"

She wiped it against her thigh. "Don't be hurt."

Lying on his side, head propped on his hand, she felt him reach out in the dark. Finding her ankle, he curved his fingers around it, stroking the hollow behind the bone. "Tell me, Gwen. It's dark. Tell me the truth."

Illogical but on target. She knew if he understood that much, he'd understand a lot of things. "I want your body—"

"But not me."

She wished he hadn't figured it out so fast. The last thing she'd ever wanted was to hurt him. "I have the best, most relaxed, happiest times with you. And you know I can't resist you when you touch me. But realistically, I can't see us—" Her voice almost cracked, so she stopped talking.

"No future at all," he repeated flatly. "Plus you don't love me. Well, that's honest at least." He rolled over on his back on the redwood slats. "Anytime you want to come over and pour lemon juice on my paper cuts, feel free."

She hiccuped and laughed. "You never stop kidding."

"And you never stop thinking. Sleep with me. See where it leads. That's all I'm asking."

Where had taking chances led her so far? She'd grown to like him better than she ever intended, her desires flamed higher than she could control. Around Dave fantasies took flight. Magic hovered overhead, whispering that anything was possible. He'd be a superb lover, attentive, skilled, inventive, and inexhaustible. If she took a chance, their lovemaking might indeed lead to love.

But not to commitment, marriage. He'd never be tied down that way.

"I don't think that's the way to a lasting relationship," she said.

Him either. He already knew he was in love—the pain pummeling his heart told him so. *Happy?* a sarcastic voice prodded him. *Here's the risky business you wanted.*

So why didn't he believe her when she turned him away? Something about those kisses, that hunger. "All kidding aside, I think you're afraid of how powerful this could be."

"Dave, I can't."

"Why?"

"I've tried. I've dated. I told myself I loved various men, but as much as one or the other fit the bill, there was always something missing. I'm not like Charlotte. I don't throw myself into grand passions. I inch along. I protect myself."

"I wouldn't hurt you."

"You'd never get close enough to try."

Brave words spoken a day too late. Dave had gotten closer with his caring, his kidding, his breath-stealing kisses, than any man she'd known. While she'd laughed at his lighthearted ways, he'd somehow edged his way inside her heart. She cared for him more than she wanted to admit. For that reason alone, she wanted to protect him.

Slipping her hand to her ankle, she twined her fingers with his. The qualities of a husband were dependability, ambitions that matched hers, and above all, commitment. Friends were for good times, alternate points of view, stimulating arguments and shared laughs.

For the sake of their friendship, she had to be rigorously honest. For the sake of dignity, she had to keep from crumbling beneath the disappointment. "You'll never know how much I prize your friendship."

"Not the 'just friends' speech, please."

"I couldn't be this honest with anyone else."

"I'll tell myself that in the morning. When I wake up alone."

"I don't want to use you, Dave."

"You were willing a minute ago."

She sighed indulgently. "Why have you been chasing me? A challenge? Boredom? Curiosity?"

Dave grimaced. If she was that hard on herself, how hard would she be on him? But part of him sprang to the dare, eager to prove himself. *Set the walls high, Lady Gweneth, so I can scale them.* Honesty was Wall One. "I chase you because this is the only way you take me seriously." He ran his hand up the back of her ankle, tickling her calf until it bunched in his palm.

The owl hooted again. It wasn't a question of "who" anymore. "Why? Why can't we be friends?" she asked.

"Why not risk being lovers?"

"Because you could be right. If we fell in love, we'd be in deeper than ever and there'd still be no future for us. You aren't really the husband type." She tried to say it gently.

After a moment, he spoke. "Loving me isn't part of your game plan, huh?"

"No. It isn't." Unprepared for the emotions rushing through her, she staggered blindly toward the door. "I'm sorry."

Inside, the house was cool and black, like a tomb. The bedroom was no better.

Loving Dave wasn't part of her life's plan. She'd known that from the start. Eyes shut against the white glare of the bathroom light, she splashed her face with water.

If she'd been a little less upright morally, she could have slept with him the first time they'd met! "But no, you had to worry about him, laugh at all his jokes. Now he thinks he loves you."

"And you love him too?" the woman in the mirror asked.

Maybe she did. "But you know damn well you can't change him."

Living day by day, seeing where things led, was not Gwen's idea of a life. She and Dave were opposites in too many ways. She had plans, intentions, goals she followed like a train on a track.

She buried her face in a towel, an image haunting her as if from a dream. What if one day she got to the station and the platform was empty?

Dave revolved on the stool in the loft, staring at the rumpled bed. Back to the drawing board, literally.

He sketched the futon. Sheets, pillows, a shading of color. All surrounding an empty hole. No heart to this picture. No body.

"*Nobody*. Huh." Amazing how the subconscious worked, he thought, puns, symbols, visual metaphors. If you clued in, you could learn a lot. Gwen's way was different. She theorized, analyzed, and arrived at conclusions as opposed to his as a financial statement was to a surreal dream.

They had one thing in common, though, they put their problems down on paper. His stared him in the face—the empty bed, the empty life.

"Promise me you'll be my friend," she'd said, stepping through the sliders into the living room.

He'd picked up some of her books and brought them in, listening to her pad across the carpet to the master bedroom. He hadn't answered. *You knew she wanted you to,* his conscience grumbled. Exactly why he'd withheld the words.

People didn't have to throw plates or slam doors to hurt each other. He and Gwen were doing fine with careful conversation and skirted issues.

So far he'd followed his instincts every step of the way where Gwen was concerned. The first time he'd kissed her, his instincts hadn't been wrong there.

And the previous weekend, when they'd arrived simultaneously, his instinct had said run, the lady's not for you. But he'd stayed, a deeper instinct had spoken, linked to the one that guided his hand, tracing the shape of a woman on the bed, legs curled in comfort, not protection, face cradled on a pillow, arm crooked.

Gwen. So deep in his mind, his heart, his soul, he could conjure her there while she slept below.

Sketching the outline of her cheek, his pencil stalled at her mouth. It often said things her tongue didn't dare.

The pencil moved faster. He got the hair right, her hands

He'd go down to her room, open the door with a nudge of his foot. She'd be sleeping, face resting on her hand. He'd bend over her and skim a kiss across her temple.

She'd stir. He'd say, "It's me."

Yes. She needed him, he'd seen it in her smudged eyes, her tired smiles, her vulnerable, needy kisses.

She'd welcome him. The emotions aroused hours before would remain, growing, seeping through her dreams. She'd be ready. All her reasons mere dust when he touched her.

He'd draw her T-shirt up, smiling at whatever the slogan on it might be. In the dark it didn't matter. In the dark, he'd kick off his shorts and slide in beside her. Between arms open and accommodating. Between legs lithe and moist. Between petals of soft swollen flesh, coating the length of him, hard and aching.

In front of the easel, he rested his hand below his waist, a throb of urgency pulsing there. It was in the picture too—the pulse, the rapid strokes. Hurry, it said.

Hunger. Passion. Possession. Once touched, she'd never say no. And once the sun came up, she'd never look at him again, never trust him, never smile or ruffle his hair.

A man had to take his chances. What rankled worst of all, he wasn't sure he was man enough to risk it. *Maybe that's why she still won't take you seriously.*

Brow dotted with sweat, eyes filmy with exhaustion—he bowed his head and conceded defeat. He'd never go to her room.

He drew a breast, cloaked beneath a short, filmy

gown. The gown was a gift, his invention. That's all he'd give her tonight, he thought.

Cursing, he tossed a charcoal pencil to the floor, wondering spitefully if somewhere in the cottage she was as wide awake as he, waiting for something neither dared claim.

Eight

Gwen brushed her teeth vigorously. She combed her wet hair, trying to decide whether to blow it dry. It would look too fluffy, she told herself, too attractive. She didn't want him thinking—

"Good heavens, woman, what else is he going to think when you wrap your legs around him so hard, you fall out of a hammock!" she said aloud.

A wry smile in the bathroom mirror didn't lift her mood any.

As she exited the master bedroom, strands of gold and purple and deep blue spilled through the stained glass window beside the front door, a rainbow in the room. David had said this place was magic, from the trees to the stones to the sky.

But the magic disappeared the moment she realized the loft was empty. The magic was Dave, what he did to her, what he made her feel, what he let her reveal. Then she saw the drawing.

A queer sensation shuddered through her. Realizing how closely he'd observed her ignited sparks beneath her skin, shivers of awareness so intense, they were almost a violation. Her shoulders stiffened at the inference she was his to depict. He'd watched her, desired her, devoured and dissected her. He'd analyzed her—in his way. She wanted to draw a blanket over the easel, or the woman pictured on the bed.

The gown he'd envisioned consisted of one line of lace across her thigh, a shadow fold at the juncture of her legs. Her breasts were heavy and full and plain to see, the aureoles rosy in sleep, a nipple defined by a faint circular line. She traced it with her finger, a strangely erotic thrill humming through her.

He'd dashed off the title, *Study,* in the corner. Gwen understood organizing thoughts on paper. But this. *Is that really how he sees me?* she wondered. The woman was sensual and, if not already sated by a lover, about to awake and become so.

The picture told her one more thing; he hadn't listened. It couldn't have been drawn by a "friend."

"Calling Norman Rockwell," she muttered, legs shaking as she inched her way down the ladder.

The sweatshirt she'd thrown on couldn't hide the body inside it, not from Dave. She'd revealed so much the night before, emotionally and physically. And apparently, she'd chased him off for good.

"Why do you do this to me?" she asked his absent spirit. He charmed her, provoked her, challenged her, giving her no goal except enjoyment. The only catch—her enjoyment seemed inextricably linked to him. Without him she hated to think how dreary life would be, how usual again, how normal.

"Oh, Dave would love that," she muttered, kicking into a run-down pair of sneakers. "Prizing the abnormal, lusting after the offbeat, his skewed point of view."

A man can't *make* you happy, she lectured, tying her shoes good and tight. The word "straitlaced" taunted her. Maybe that's why she'd always avoided him. One week with Dave, and parts of her were coaxed to the surface she'd kept buried for years.

She swung open the side door to a gaping black square of asphalt. His car was gone. Her heart sank and her bottom hit the top step of the deck.

"Hi."

She jumped inwardly, sweeping her bangs off her forehead and finding no glasses there. She gazed at the tall beige blur and blinked.

Dave twisted the hose nozzle and soaked his head in cold water. His running shorts were drenched with sweat, his body glistening. "Going running?" he asked, eyeing her sneakers.

She'd never run so much as a city block. She dusted off her shorts and said, "Sure!"

His presence not only encouraged her to reach for new experiences, now he had her volunteering for a torture she'd successfully avoided for thirty-four years. "Cellulite never sleeps, you know. Join me?"

He considered a minute, his Adam's apple bobbing as he drank from the hose. She wasn't surprised when he trotted up beside her. Dave chose what he wanted and when; he prized his freedom.

An exciting thought when he chose to be with her; terrifying, too, to think he might choose otherwise someday.

A half mile down the road, she eased up on running when a host of wheezing noises joined a cramp in her side. She slowed to a fast walk. "Do you meet a lot of girls this way?" she asked conversationally.

"Fair amount."

With a towel slung over his shoulders, hands resting on slim hips, he probably led women down Malibu beach like the Pied Piper of Hamelin.

His cooldown was her Bataan death march. She sprinted to the next curve. The sharp sunlight made the far-off mountain peaks crystal clear, each pine a wire brush against a flat blue sky.

"Then why me?" Gwen asked.

He took a minute to answer, bending to pick up a glittering piece of quartz. He tossed it at a tree trunk. "Would you believe it if I said I don't know?" Probably, Dave thought. She already thought he was shallow as a satellite dish. "My instincts say go. We fit."

The arm he draped around her shoulders emphasized their difference in height. The arm she slid around his lower back emphasized their difference in width. She nodded toward the shadows loping along in front of them. "Doesn't look like a perfect couple to me."

"Look inside."

"To what? Our careers, our attitudes, our values?"

"What do you think I value?"

"Fun."

"True. Go for two."

"Your freedom."

"True again. The lady's gonna win a prize in a minute. Don't you? Value freedom, that is."

"When it comes to a relationship, I value commitment."

He matched his stride to hers. "Are you asking me for one?"

Her mother had always warned her she'd do what she did now: She tripped on her own shadow. "I was trying to show you how far apart we are."

"I don't see that at all." He swung her into his arms, face to face, body to body. The sweatshirt didn't protect her from the heat of him, from lips that knew hers too well.

She breathed his name. "Please, don't."

"We agree on a number of things. On the hammock," he nuzzled her cheek, "on the deck, on the dirt beneath the house." He slipped a kiss in under her hair. "I bet we'd even agree on a bed, if you'd let me."

Her legs quaked as if she'd run a marathon. The oxygen flowed so thinly in her blood, she barely felt her heart beat anymore. "I saw the sketch."

He looked in her eyes. "What did you think?"

"There's more to you than this happy-go-lucky guy."

"Honey, you just hit the jackpot." He swung her slowly around in a kiss that was half bear hug, half seduction. "We're getting there."

"Where?"

"Wherever we're going."

"And where is that?"

"I can't draw you a map."

"I need to know."

"Know this."

She moaned when his tongue plunged into her mouth. "This is no way to solve an argument," she managed to say a moment later.

"Is that what we're having? Call Rob and Charlotte, they oughta see this." He kissed her again, on the corner of her smile, in the middle of the road. Then he brushed her lower body with his and felt her quiver. "On second thought, maybe we'll keep this part to ourselves. What's the matter?"

"You make me laugh when I want to cry."

"About what?"

"You shouldn't take this too seriously."

"You never took me seriously before."

"I'm talking about a future."

"About giving up on one."

"Just don't expect more, Dave. The here and now is all we have."

Somewhere along the way, his Lady Gweneth had learned all his lines. Their shallowness stung. Did she fear that if she didn't say them, he would?

Before he asked, she pulled his head down to hers for another kiss, her fingers gripping the back of his neck. The strength of her need shook him. And he heard himself making promises he'd never made before.

She wasn't listening.

"Come with me to the house."

She nodded, pressing her cheek to his chest and hearing his heart beat.

In an instant they were running, Dave jogging and laughing encouragement.

"David King, you are one kinky character," she huffed.

"Why? Because I want to get you home?"

"Watching me chug up this slope is nobody's idea of erotica."

He grinned from ear to ear and swiped a handful of damp hair off his forehead. "Wanna bet?"

She shook her head. He'd already seen her body in the fading light the night before and in his imagination. That thought should have worried her. Somehow it didn't. Dave with his sinewy build frankly enjoyed her rounder form. No telling how or why. His thought processes were as mysterious as ever.

But his caring, his attentiveness, his loneliness weren't mysterious. He liked to go off and draw while she studied, but the image of him summoning a woman with strokes of chalk made her ache. If she had to out-Bara Theda Bara, out-belly Beli-Zar, she'd love him as no other woman or girl ever had.

He might not fill every requirement she demanded of a husband, but as a lover she knew he'd be more than she ever dared dream. With Dave, she dared.

He let her shower alone, though they both sensed the risk of second thoughts. Freedom to choose, she thought. He gave her that, and the freedom to be a woman she was just beginning to know.

"Some freedom." Gwen laughed when she found him guarding the bathroom door. He'd swiped every towel from the linen closet inside, probably while she'd soaped her hair, before commencing sentry duty.

"Thought you'd want something to wear." A white linen shirt dangled from his hand.

She reached around the bathroom door, pointedly ignoring the way he glanced over her head to the mirrors behind her. "Thanks."

Kicking the door shut behind her, she shrugged into the shirt and gave a squeak. "David, behave!" But it wasn't him; the hem had caught in the door.

"You got X-ray vision?" he called from the bed.

Her cheeks flushed. "Never mind." The shirt hung to her mid-thighs. She wore nothing else. He'd swiped her dirty clothes as well.

Opening the door, he grinned appreciatively, scanning her toes, her knees, the hem of the shirt. "Upstairs?"

They climbed the ladder, Dave planting kisses in the small of her back, her fingers clutching the rungs in response.

"I'm a klutz, don't forget."

"I won't let you fall."

She already had, in love with him. But she would never, ever use it to tie him down, not Dave, not her free spirit.

Besides, he listened this time. To prevent them both toppling to the floor, he sensibly avoided touching the downy back of her thigh until they reached the top.

Dave unrolled the futon across the corner of the loft. Gwen sat on its low edge, her knees chest-high. He knelt behind her, tapping her shoulder as if he had some secret to impart. When she turned her head, he kissed her cheek, wrapped his arms around her waist, under her breasts. The cotton shirt grazed up her legs, which were sprinkled with fine golden hair and droplets of water.

The sated woman on the easel lay curled in sleep.

"This isn't what you sketched me in," Gwen murmured, referring to the shirt.

"Reality's always better than imagination."

"Is it? I'd pale against all your bright colors, your action and adventure."

"Maybe I like pale."

She shuddered in reply when he rasped his cheek across the nape of her neck. She bowed her head and gave over to the sensation.

He followed a drop of water from her temple to her jaw, her throat to her collarbone. Her breasts showed darkly through the wet transparent shirt. "Let me cling here," he whispered, plucking the fabric away from her rapidly tightening nipples. Reaching inside, he covered her abdomen with the flat of his hand and pressed.

She grasped his hand, holding it to her, relishing the intensity and halting, for a moment, his urge to go further.

He got the message. Leaning back, he peeled the shirt from her spine, lifting it away to reveal the soft indentation he'd pressed his lips to on the ladder.

"Stuffy up here," he said softly.

She laughed. Or gasped. He wasn't sure. He'd kiss her again and find out.

"I can't breathe when you do that," she whispered.

"I could turn on the fan." The overhead blades would cut the light to shadows, stirring the air on her damp skin. Like the alternating streaks of dried sweat and tap water on his skin. He should've joined her in the shower. If he had, they'd never have made it up to the loft.

"Dave?"

He paused.

She turned, folding her legs under her, kneeling to face him. "Tell me what you want."

"I said last night we'd do whatever you wanted." *And nothing she didn't.*

"I want to know what you want." He couldn't give her a lifetime commitment, she was grown-up enough to face that, to recognize fairy-tale endings for what they were. But she could thank him for the sweetness, the sensations, even the danger—for letting her risk a little more than she might have dared alone.

She might not tell him she loved him, but she could show him how precious he was to her, always had been. "What do *you* want?"

His eyes flashed with that piercing concentration she'd seen him lavish on his work, on anything, she suspected, that mattered to him. "Touch me," he said hoarsely.

His muscles bunched when she complied, glistening from his run, the dry heat of the loft. She ran her hands down his chest, up a knotted thigh and under the skimpy shorts. His stomach rippled, his lips thinned.

Gwen wasn't shy. Not when she pursued the things she wanted. *Want me,* he moaned silently. *Me.*

His body bucked when her fingertips skimmed his taut intimate skin, exploring in the tangles of his coiled hair.

His hand clamped on hers, his eyes unfocused, his jaw set. "You're going to make me crazy."

She rose on her knees and kissed him softly on the lips, her unbuttoned shirt wafting open. "You've done so much for me. I never told you how much I appreciated it."

"Thanks." He gulped. "But give me a minute."

Too many thoughts rammed through his head, emotions he hadn't planned on dealing with, not now, not when he wanted to concentrate on the delicate curves of her freckled flesh, the vulnerable softness of mounds and hollows.

It wasn't a matter of sex. It was Gwen. Living up to her expectations. Not living up to her image of him as an overcharged younger man. He wanted to take his time. But if she didn't stop ministering to him in that knee-buckling, throat-clenching way, he'd explode right there. Poised on the crest of a monster roller coaster, he knew the climax would be swift, the drop dazzling, awesome.

But they had to get there together.

He lifted her hand from danger, laving her palm with his tongue until she parted her lips and inhaled short and sharp. As if asking her to dance, he wrapped his other arm around her back and hauled her to him.

He hummed "Moondance." She smelled and tasted of soap, he of salt.

Since he held her left hand, she spider-walked her right up his arm to tickle his earlobe.

"Gwen."

A sultry smile. "You rang?"

"You're having fun with me."

"You bet I am." She was almost drunk on it, a genie

escaped from a bottle. "Is this a new game? We only touch from the neck down?"

"Could be."

Just because she'd feared loving him didn't mean she didn't know how. What she did next had him exhaling on a groan, gulping down a yelp of sheer delight. "Lady, you are great."

"And you're sweet."

He paused.

"I wonder," she said, tilting her head to the side, "if you'd be as sweet everywhere else."

He edged back on his knees, body held rigid while the tip of her tongue flicked against his shoulder, his chest, his lowest rib. "Hold that thought," he croaked, holding his breath.

He practically stumbled to the dresser beside the bed. Purposely, he tore open a box, ignoring how Gwen reclined catlike on the futon, kicking sheets away, shrugging out of his shirt, revealing a perfectly rounded shoulder as sexy in its unveiling as any Venus.

Except Venus lacked arms. What Gwen did with her hands—

Stroking on a condom, Dave knew she'd be willing to do the honors but seriously doubted there'd be any need for it by the time she finished. Arms outstretched, he gripped the dresser's edge and fought for control.

"Dave?"

His back muscles flexed, all the way down to places that, Gwen knew, weren't technically part of the back. The muscles tightened all the same. She couldn't imagine why he'd be insecure. There was always the possibility that her body didn't excite him—

She tossed that thought on the floor with the last pillow. When Dave turned, his face gaunt with desire, she knew she wasn't the problem. "Coming to bed?"

He stretched the length of it, gathering her in his arms. For a long time he kissed her, proving to himself, to her, he could take his time.

Until she said, "Touch me," and the frank plea coursed through him like fire.

He touched her. After a moment, she begged him to kiss her the same way.

It shouldn't have surprised him, or rocked him so. She was the Gwen he'd wanted, a woman who didn't and wouldn't play games, blunt and honest enough to tell him they had no future. He had one chance to prove her wrong.

So he kissed her, drinking her in, urging her higher, faster. He'd take everything she had. Her freedom, her vulnerability, was sexier than hell. She stirred him like no other woman had.

She threw her head back on the pillow, reaching blindly for him. He touched her cheek. She kissed his palm, his thumb, taking his fingers in her mouth and suckling them one by one.

He couldn't say stop, slow down. Couldn't say anything when she curled her legs around him, nudging the backs of his thighs with her heels. Her breasts skimmed his nipples, her tongue raked them. His tip touched her milky core, and his jaw clamped shut until it hurt. If he'd counted on the latex to dull the sensation, it was flimsy protection indeed.

Blood pounded in his ears as she impelled him forward, deeper. She undulated like a river, and he slipped inside.

His lungs ached with the effort. The room spun. He'd broken out in a chilly sweat. He wanted to think, for her sake. To pull back and lave her again with his tongue, but she insisted, his own body concurred, setting up a throbbing motion of its own. Swelling, explicit, intense.

It happened fast. An incredible rush surged through him, a series of driving thrusts, exploding, her name echoing harshly in the fallout, the shuddering silence.

Gwen waited until the tension left him, wrenching his body with such powerful aftershocks, she could do nothing but receive and rejoice. They lay quiet, one of them spent. He moved again. She stopped him.

Eyes shut against a rivulet of sweat on his brow, Dave turned his head. "Damn."

She kissed his temple. He flinched. He heard her breath catch.

He splayed a wide hand on her waist, sliding up to cup her with a rough squeeze. "I'm sorry." He brushed his thumb over her breast. The feather-stuffed futon let out a sigh when he rolled over and stared at the ceiling.

He cursed, not bothering to hide it. Why should he? There weren't too many ways to cover up the fact he'd lost it. He dragged the sheet over his middle.

High school kids had better control. If only she hadn't—no, he couldn't blame her. Gwen was clearly a more experienced woman than he'd given her credit for, and he'd blown it, but good.

He'd thought the bedroom was the only place he'd prove himself more man than boy. Instead of being immature, he was premature!

The one thing, the *only* thing that could make it worse, would be if she understood.

"Anything I can do?"

"Don't be *kind*," he said tensely.

She'd adopted the position in the sketch, curled on her side, a hand under her cheek. Unlike the woman in the portrait, whose lids were demurely lowered, hers were open as she watched him, her eyes the color of the golden slats of wood that made up the peaked roof.

He would've scowled at what sounded like a chuckle from her, but that would've meant opening his eyes. She brushed her hand up his chest. He held it down with his own. *Dammit, Gwen, don't leave me. I'll do better next time.*

She sat up. The shirt tangled around her elbows. Her hair hung in tendrils, half wet from the shower he should have taken with her.

"Give me a minute." He sat up, grabbed his shorts

from beside the mattress, and headed downstairs. Ten minutes later he was back, rinsed from a quick shower but hotter than ever, wiped out.

He scrounged through the dresser, tossing unwanted items on the floor, deliberately ignoring the box of condoms in the corner. He found a cleaner pair of running shorts, another shirt. Slinging it on, he didn't bother with buttons.

All that time, she said nothing. No disappointment. No blame. No begging for more. And, thank the Amazon Goddess of Love, no worldly-wise encouragement.

Safely ensconced behind his easel, he got up the guts to look at her. Her eyes were closed. He studied the woman he'd drawn. Picking up an eraser from habit, he rubbed out the lace across her thigh and added a thicker line, a shirt hem. Buttons and buttonholes darted in and out of the rise and fall of her breasts.

She let him draw. No more was said.

Fifteen minutes passed. Her body tingled with the waning of desire, still marked by his touch.

She got off the bed and came over behind him, her shirt half opened, her body skimming his back.

"No excuses," he said harshly.

"How about compliments?"

He frowned.

Without noticing, she'd begun kneading the tension in his shoulders. Gwen had learned a lot about tension in her life. Dave had shown her a dozen ways to ease it. He hurt. She helped him.

He shrugged her hand off his shoulder and returned to his picture. "Don't hover, please." He could have stabbed her with a pen point. He bowed his head and huffed a long breath. "Sorry. I need space."

"Freedom. I know."

"What do you know?"

"That we couldn't handle this, not long-term. You'd push me away sooner or later—if you ever made the mistake of making a long-term commitment."

"Gwen."

"It's better we face it now. That doesn't mean we can't hold on to what we have." She did. She curled her fingers into the streak of muscle atop his shoulder blades.

"You think sex is all we have?" Hell, he'd been trying to show her he loved her.

"To think a man would be so on fire for me he couldn't stop . . . That was the most exciting thing I've ever—"

"I wanted to—"

"To what?" She touched his face, spun him toward her on the stool.

"To prove I wasn't the boy you take me for."

She laughed softly. Twining her fingers in his hair, she examined the flickering gold. "You're an impossibly sexy man. Why do you think I tried so hard to pretend you weren't?"

He kissed her palm as she trailed it over his lips. Precious, giving. This was the Gwen he knew no other man had seen. Disheveled, rumpled. His pride flared at the flush spreading across her chest. He'd put it there.

He grasped her to him, her breasts even with his mouth. "I wanted to show you."

She chuckled. "I'd say you did."

"Hardly."

"The first time—"

"Don't say it."

"I wanted it that way," she insisted.

"You planned that?"

She laughed. "Nobody plans all that. But I wanted to give you something. Didn't you like it?"

Disingenuous minx. He stood, tempering her sass for a minute with sheer size. "I wanted to give you something too."

"Something I'll remember all my life."

"We can make it, Gwen. The two of us. We just have to take it as it comes. Lie back down."

Her brows rose. "So soon?"

He swatted her on the fanny. "You there, me here."

"Imaginative to say the least."

He rested his backside on the stool's edge. "Open your shirt, just a little."

Reclining on the futon, she did as told, trembling at the intimacy of posing, scrutinized by those probing eyes. He saw every inch, rendered it, and she feared, recognized the love she couldn't ask him to return. Her mouth curved ruefully at the irony. What she loved in him was precisely the freedom she lacked in herself. And the reason she could never ask him to change.

Nine

She set the empty bowl of vegetable soup beside the bed. They'd eaten in style with the sheet as their tablecloth, sprawling on the wooden floor.

Dave had pretended to go on drawing when she'd gone down to make lunch. But Gwen could've sworn she heard him pacing in his bare feet, stretching the kinks out of his back, frowning.

Yes, you could hear a frown, she thought. It sounded like clenched teeth, huffed breaths, swallowed curses.

The soup was gone, the dishes stacked beside the ladder. "Don't carry that down, I'll get it," he'd said in sweet consideration for her safety. Then he'd gone back to his easel.

She posed willingly; talking seemed to have become difficult. So she stretched on the bed, legs elongated, a pillow held to her breasts, and let him draw. Eventually her breasts grew tender from brushing the brocade as she breathed, achy with wanting something else. She hadn't questioned why he wanted the prop, then it had dawned on her.

You son-of-a-gun, you're hiding and you expect me to do the same. He had his easel; he'd given her that silly pillow.

Slipping off the futon, she waltzed over, braving his

scowl when she broke her pose. Naked, she came nearer. "This is very sexy," she noted, "being observed. Having someone really see you. I feel vulnerable."

She didn't act it, Dave thought, as her hand slid up his arm.

"Staring is an intimate act," he said. "That's why lovers trade long looks." They traded one of their own.

She didn't say it. Neither did he. The part about being lovers.

He put the charcoal down. "You going to keep touching me?"

"I hope so," she replied softly.

"What about the pose?"

"No more poses."

She took his face in her hands and kissed him, mouth and tongue, an erotic exploration that left no doubt who was older, who wanted to take charge. She offered him a dare.

"I'll be damned," Dave muttered. Standing, he pulled her into his arms and returned the favor. If she thought she was being "nice" to him, "encouraging poor, sweet Dave," he'd disabuse her of that notion but fast.

His fingers darkened her arms with charcoal smudges that looked like bruises. That shocked him to a halt. Abruptly, he set her away from him. "In the mood I'm in, I'd hurt you."

"In the mood I'm in, I might like it."

He closed his eyes and swallowed. "Gwen, don't say things like that."

"Too much?" Her knowingness crumbled a bit, revealing the nerve it had taken her to walk over stone naked and stone beautiful.

"Too good," he smiled, his chest heaving in a deep sigh. He shook his head. "I knew when I kissed you it'd be hot, never this hot. Shows what I get for underestimating you."

They traded kisses and touches and whispered

words. Gwen's heart soared at how easy it was this time. No fears, no doubts. Anything she asked, Dave accepted.

Like a freight train, they gathered speed, slowly building, hisses of indrawn breaths like brakes, sparks spitting off the tracks as hands caressed. A picture of a train entering a dark tunnel occurred to her, and she laughed at the glaring symbolism, sharing it with Dave.

"I'm not the only one with a skewed sense of humor," he retorted.

"Or a visual imagination."

"If you say anything about the little engine that could, I'll spank you."

They laughed for minutes, tussling in the sheets, until a glancing touch made her hesitate, her eyes flutter shut. "You know what I think of when I think of trains? Distant whistles in the night, making me wish I was going somewhere. But they're lonely too. Nothing lonelier than a train's whistle." Unless it was Dave, creating at his easel what was there for the asking.

He kissed her, gathering her body back to his. "I love you, Gwen." He watched her lips compress as he slid into her, felt her hand tighten on his arm. He repeated the words.

"Love me," she asked.

In a dozen ways, he did.

It was more than trains and tracks and tunnels, more than metaphors. It was rhythm, an escalating thrumming pulsing through her blood and his, a piston moving them forward and higher, climbing, rising, reaching, and finding. Two people moving as one. A sharp cry caught in her throat as she got there first, shuddering down and down and up again as he joined her on that plateau, the pumping energy of his body cleaving hers, clutching hers, whispering dark, searing permanent words.

"Gwen. Come with me. Love me."

"I will."

• • •

"You've got the greatest skin," he said.

Gwen smiled shyly, tugging the hem of the shirt down her thigh.

"Keep it there," he ordered.

"Bossy."

He grinned, a brassy, bet-your-buttons grin that could charm money from a miser. Or caution from a woman with an ounce of sense. Gwen seemed to have mislaid hers.

She laughed and lay back. He wanted her in repose. She'd give it to him. She'd give David just about anything. And he'd take it, no strings.

And if I want strings? she thought. They hadn't spoken of commitment.

She smiled to herself to think how completely things turned around. She used to hold Dave's carefree ways against him. Now, having learned to relish the moment in his arms, she loved him for it. He'd released her from all her chains.

I love him, she thought quietly.

And you can lose him, came the silent reply.

She refused to doubt. For one day he was hers.

And tomorrow? The words faded with the doubts as she drifted off to sleep.

Gwen never took afternoon naps. Then again, she'd never made love in the middle of the day before. A shame, she thought, awareness filtering into her dream like the slanted afternoon light. That meant she'd never awakened to something as stirring as Dave beside her, or as peaceful, or as necessary.

"Dreaming?"

She ran her tongue over her teeth. He offered her the beer he balanced on his lap, long legs stretched beside her, back against the wall. He'd cleared away the dishes and wrapped up his work for the day.

She took a sip. "How did you get here?"

"You don't remember? I'm crushed."

"I meant next to me. Under me."

Without waking her, he'd managed to maneuver her head onto his chest, her arm thrown casually across his waist. As if she belonged there. She knew from the heat in her cheek that she'd rested her ear above his heart for a while.

"I didn't talk in my sleep, did I?"

"Yep."

She blanched. The remnants of her dream had left her wanting and restless and a tad irritated. Well, no wonder! Her thigh diagonally straddled his, her calf resting in the space between his legs as he strummed her bare hip with his thumb as if it were a Spanish guitar—hand polished, tightly strung. "And I said?"

Dave took a swig of his beer, his throat working. "Something about fiscal years and limited yields. And interest. Compounded." He rasped that last word, voice husky and low.

A pillow came in handy for swatting purposes. "That's for being a smart aleck."

"In the mood for a fight, lady fair?" He lifted the sheet he'd draped across her as she slept.

She was in the mood, but not for that. When Dave set aside his bottle and scooted under the sheets, her head spun. But her pulse kept excellent time.

He shucked his shirt, the satiny running shorts slick against her skin. "I've been waiting two hours for you to wake up and kiss me. You must have been worn out."

"I may be . . . oh." He nipped her neck. "If we do this again."

"Try it and find out, that's my motto."

A delightful buzz sang through her body. She loved him so much. And she'd slept away the afternoon. Strangely, she felt no need to apologize, or to live up to his expectations, or cover the sags he pretended not to notice.

He loved her as is. As hard as it would be to lose him, she'd do him the honor of loving him the same way. Freely, without strings.

Forever, her heart whispered.

• • •

"There is a gap, we can't deny it."

The age gap. Gwen broached the subject the next evening.

They'd spent a night in bed, a morning pursuing their separate vocations within three feet of each other on the deck, and an afternoon frolicking in frigid Lake Tahoe. Now she sat swamped in sweaters on the hammock while he played suburban husband by shish-kabobbing a row of Cornish hens.

Living with someone, growing old with them, wasn't a matter of playing house. Love was serious business. Gwen wanted to put Dave's feet back on the ground, gently, and see which path he chose.

"Those are just years on a calendar," he said. "What's inside is what counts."

"You think we match inside?"

He waggled his brows in her direction. "I've been inside. I thought it was a great fit."

"Be serious. I've been organized since I was five and put all my crayons in the proper slots." She glanced at the pastels he'd carted downstairs, broken off stubs tossed on top of each other, the box lid canted against the drawing pad alongside the rubber band that held it all in place.

"People don't change, Dave. The surest way to ruin a marriage is secretly hoping they will."

"But people grow, and grow up. Love means learning another person. Bending a bit."

"And Charlotte and Robert?"

"They prove my point in reverse. In a relationship, you give a little to save what's important."

"Which is?"

"The relationship itself. Two staying together are more important than one being right."

"Do you have to be so mature when I'm trying to preach?"

"Surprised you, huh?"

"I guess *Sewer Screams* never prepared me for a sensible, mature you."

"You're sensible enough for ten couples."

"I won't be Wendy to your Peter Pan."

"Have I ever asked you to mother me? I've been trying for years to get you to see me as just the opposite!" He lowered his voice and squirted starter fluid on the dying coals.

"Watch it, that could explode."

"Yes, Mother."

Gwen bit her lip. "Are we having our first argument?"

Dave looked up. "How many rules have we broken?"

Gwen blushed, remembering his reaction to her *Fighting Fair* list. "We dragged up the past."

"We did that. Next?"

"Name calling."

"I haven't."

"'Mother'? In that snide tone?"

"The urges I have for you only Oedipus could appreciate. Wasn't there another?"

"Don't go to bed angry."

"So we have to settle this now." He eased in, sitting facing her in the hammock, his ankles on either side of her hips. "Remember something about touching during an argument? Harder to stay mad that way."

"I'm not mad. I can't realistically see us planning a life together."

"Neither can I. Like John Lennon said, 'Life is what happens while you're making other plans.' What do you say we have a life, Gwen, together?"

Her heart clutched. If only he meant it. "What about marriage?" she asked.

He shook his head. "Not when I see what Rob got himself into. Not that I blame Charlotte, they made their hell together. Same as my parents."

"They divorced, didn't they?"

"I think they're the reason Rob's so paranoid about Charlotte tearing him apart in court. My parents made a career of it."

Gwen had heard the story from Charlotte, but always in relation to Robert. She'd never really thought of the effect his parent's tumultuous divorce must have had on Dave. She'd never suspected. He acted as if deep emotions rolled off him. He'd fooled a lot of people that way, including her. "How did you feel about it?"

"Well, doc—"

"I mean it."

Dave shrugged and tilted his head back to watch the stars wink. "It didn't affect us much."

"How can you say that?"

"We didn't live with Dad's drinking. Not when it was bad. And we were too young to know about the fooling around."

But they'd lived with the consequences, Gwen thought. The anger and accusations. "Boys need a father. How did you cope?"

"Can't you guess?" He nodded at the stack of comic books he'd bought in town. "I'm forever stuck at a mental age of eleven, creating worlds boys can get lost in."

"Didn't one of your heroes fight alcoholism? Victor."

Dave grinned, pleased she'd remembered. "Victor hurled a wrecking ball at Blackjack's getaway car."

Gwen joined in. "But the Cape of Judgment blew in his eyes and he hit a school bus instead."

"No one was hurt, but the near tragedy drove him to the *Days of Whine and Neuroses*."

She pinched his leg.

"But seriously, folks. With a superhero's willpower, he worked his way through it. Those tights drew some funny looks at AA meetings though," Dave added with a smirk.

She laughed because he meant her to.

"What are you thinking, Oh mighty brain? You've got that wrinkle between your brows."

"I was thinking," she replied carefully, "that you

exaggerate pain and then create characters who can master it."

"Uh-oh. Analysis dead ahead."

"I use lists to get my life in control. You color it the way you want it."

"Deep. And accurate. But wrong in one major respect." He massaged her ankle. "I don't just color it, I pencil and ink it too."

"So kid about it."

He fully intended to. But some things made a man ponder the intractable things in life. Like being alone. Like finding a woman to let in. "What would you say if, every morning, I asked you to be mine for today and today alone?"

"I'd say, 'What about tomorrow?'"

It was so typical, they both laughed.

"Always thinking ahead," he chided.

"That's how you get what you want."

"Love is a gift. You can't order it from a catalogue."

"So I've discovered."

"People love each other all the time without marriage. Live-ins. Paramours. Lovers."

The way he said the last word made her look up. They were already lovers.

She shook her head, a lump refusing to leave her throat. "Not me. I'm the marrying kind."

"No POSSLQs?" he asked.

"Huh?"

"Persons of the Opposite Sex Sharing Living Quarters. I tried to draw one once. Hairy hunchbacked thing with a long tail—my POSSLQ. Kind of cuddly, though. Didn't catch on."

"I want to get serious."

So did he. He'd talked change and growth a minute earlier. He'd scaled this mountain looking for something that wasn't entirely his creation or within his control. And she'd seen right through him. "I can be as committed as anybody," he said.

"Really?"

She didn't sound as if she believed him. He wasn't

sure he believed himself. "Freedom to me means I'll never drive myself so hard, or count on anything so much that I'd kill myself over losing it. Whether it's a business or a busted marriage."

"The way your father did."

"Like him. There's commitment and there's obsession, Gwen. There has to be a point where you can walk away."

They sat in silence a moment. The hammock swayed.

"I noticed you've successfully escaped marriage," he said, running his hand down the front of her foot, balancing her heel on the inside of his thigh.

"I never found the right man." She looked at him and scowled, then laughed. "I have a list, okay?"

"Why am I not surprised?"

She almost threw the pillow at him, relieved for a moment to be teased again.

"Uh-uh, no hitting. Rule Ten of *Fighting Fair*."

She clutched the pillow to her chest, not questioning why she needed it now. "Mom and Dad fought so hard, so loud, and so often, I determined at the ripe age of twelve that I'd never make their mistakes."

"Sounds familiar."

"I'd sit with Mom at the kitchen table after he'd stormed out and talk it over. The mediator, the referee."

"And you made lists."

"And stuck to them. Mom never could. She'd vow never to take him back, make all kinds of promises, then he'd charm his way into the house in a week or two, and it'd start all over."

"So you never found a man who could live up to your prerequisites." If Dave hadn't been so busy kneading her arch and counting her toes, he'd have patted himself on the back for his sound conclusion.

She curled her toes around his finger. "Actually, I've found a number."

Her simple statement landed on him like a battering ram. *Boom!* While he'd buzzed around her like a gnat at family parties, getting swatted more often than not, she'd been contemplating marriage to men he hadn't even known about. "So what happened?"

She gave a big shrug, her soft brown eyes growing wide. "I don't know. They met all the specifications, but they bored me. Or I bored them. There is such a thing as being too well matched. No surprises, no adventure."

He cocked his ear as if hearing a far-off sound. A lonely coyote yelling "Yahoo" at the top of his lungs. "I believe that's the red-crested, full-breasted, 'I told you so' singing in the distance."

"Don't mock me."

"You admit opposites have their advantages."

"Did I?"

"Here, try this. You squeezed all the life out of that one."

The tassel on his pillow was gold, the trim braided with red and aqua, the brocade Indian and ornate. "Do you carry exotica around, or does it collect in your vicinity like lint?" She asked.

"Live dangerously."

"Looks like Charlotte's East Indian decor."

"Where was she during all this?"

"In my childhood? Throwing a fit, I suppose. Charlotte acts out."

"You don't say."

She was saying too much. Revealing too much. Something about his even, unjudging concentration made it easy to talk, the words falling on the evening air like motes of dust in an attic, kicked up as she shuffled through the past.

Dave didn't judge or blame. He cared without clinging, was loyal but stubbornly independent. He didn't fly off the handle. The list got longer.

Gwen quailed to think she still carried one around in her head. Caution reigned. She had to be sure, absolutely, heart-stoppingly sure before making a commitment that he'd return it. She wanted chains, ties, papers, and vows. She wanted him to love her, and she wanted it in writing.

Her heart stumbled, and her hands pressed the pillow as she caught him staring at her.

"I can't imagine you and Charlotte related."

"A week after they brought her home from the hospital, I took Mom aside and suggested, in all seriousness, they take her back and get another."

"You didn't!"

"I think Charlotte still holds it against me." She shook her head and laughed. "You just had to look at her cross-eyed in her bassinet, and she'd cry. We walked on eggshells around her."

"And around your Dad. So the family mediator became the dutiful, steady daughter times two."

"You're going to be drawing me in a librarian suit with a bun and a clipboard next. I'm not *that* repressed."

"Don't I know it." He grinned, recalling the drawing upstairs on his easel. That woman was bare everywhere, except for a pillow over her breasts, as if protecting the heart of her, a vulnerable core. Proof positive that covered could be sexier than nude. "I bet there are sides to you Charlotte's never imagined."

"Oh no. Charlotte believes every woman can be multiorgasmic. Though whether that's before or after one rediscovers one's Inner Child, I can never remember."

They both laughed.

"Crazy or not, she is my sister."

"Broken families stick together."

"You and Robert have."

"He's a great guy when he's not prosecuting his nearest and dearest."

"If you hadn't been here, I don't know what I'd have done with them. Allies come in handy."

"I've been trying to tell you we'd be great together."

"You proved that upstairs. You're precious. No, I mean that. Precious to me." She groped for the words, the ones that mattered most. "I love you."

He looked at her lips, her eyes.

For a second she couldn't repeat it, so she chattered on, "You're a great friend, supportive, funny. I've hardly worried about my test at all. I'll pass it, I think."

"Because you've studied for it twice."

"Because you've given my mind a rest from it."

"And your body a workout."

"Honestly. You're mature and thoughtful and talented and—"

"Making a new list?"

She laughed as he rearranged them on the hammock and tugged her alongside him.

"'How do I love thee, let me count the ways,'" he quoted. A kiss was One. Another kiss Two. Simple as one-two-three, he thought, the way love was supposed to be.

Although there was nothing simple about pleasing a woman on guard, the challenge held rewards he hadn't imagined.

Not a bad way to spend a lifetime, he mused, letting her show him exactly how much she loved him.

Gwen had to be back at work on Monday, three days away. The end of the week neared. Except for a few cryptic calls from Robert, a shrill one from Charlotte, and a handful of long-suffering ones from her mother and Dave's grandmother, the battle raged in Long Beach at the ocean's edge, far from the pine-covered mountains.

She and Dave had made no plans for the future. Dave didn't make plans. Soft conversation after tender lovemaking was as close as they'd come.

"I don't want what my parents had," she said. "Dad ran around, refused to pay support. There was no commitment."

Dave gave her a squeeze. "My parents had too much. They couldn't let go. Even after the divorce they had to claw at each other in court."

"What do we have?" she'd asked. "Too much or not enough?"

"We have an agreement. If we fight, we fight fair. No old resentments, no name calling."

"The whole list."

"Yeah. We'll live by your list."

"And what do I give up in this negotiation?"

His voice was soft, tender. "Don't ask me to marry you, Gwen. I'll love you as long as I live. I promise you that. I'll give you every day you want to be with me. But I give it freely. Don't ask for more."

Kissing him, she closed her eyes. It kept the tears in. "I don't want to force you to love me. This isn't emotional blackmail."

"Then promise me today, just today."

She did. And every day thereafter when they awoke, he asked for that one day and she gave it, loving him more and more, fearing only the day he stopped asking.

She promised herself no tears when that day came. No rages. Above all, no Charlottelike scenes. They would share love on his terms. But when she left, it would be on hers.

Ten

"Stay right there," Charlotte ordered.

Holding the phone to her bare breast, blushing as if Charlotte could see it, Gwen buried the receiver under her pillow and kneed Dave in the behind.

"Huh?" he grumbled in his sleep.

"Up!"

"Babe, I didn't know you could be so demanding." He rolled over, stretching a tentaclelike arm her way.

She ducked out of his bleary-eyed reach and scooted to the far side of the king-size bed in the master bedroom. "Charlotte's coming! The Human Hurricane. The Fiery Fury."

"You just gave me two terrific ideas for comic books."

Gwen listened to the garbled sound of Charlotte's voice penetrating the pillow. "We have to decide what we're going to do."

"Mmm. I'm saying good morning first." Grasping her waist, he planted a kiss smack in the middle of her abdomen.

Gwen shuddered deep inside. When she opened her eyes, his grin made her smile. "Good morning, you."

He laid his cheek against her smooth skin. "Promise me today."

A warmth suffused her, making her limbs heavy, sending tiny chills across her flesh. "I promise you today."

"Now see what Charlotte wants before she burns a hole in the pillow."

Gwen dragged out the phone, having gotten tangled in the cord somehow.

"What was that all about?" her sister demanded.

"Getting some clothes on. It's—" She gulped. It was nine-thirty, too late to complain of being awoken. "It's chilly in here."

"Well it's going to be hotter than Hades when I show you what I found."

"What?"

"Stay there and find out. And Gwen, keep Dave nearby."

"Click." Supplying the sound effects, Dave rubbed his eyes and sighed. "She even hangs up loud."

"They *are* trying to swindle me! See for yourself."

Clad in a muumuu of purples and aquas with starbursts of gold, Charlotte looked like a volcano at sunset—black hair spewing forth where smoke plumes should be, lava-red rivulets running down her fluttering sleeves. She hauled an armload of books out of her car and loaded them into Gwen's outstretched arms. A bucket brigade at a three-alarm fire couldn't have moved with more purpose. In minutes a stack of ledgers covered in dark red leather tumbled across the dining room table.

Gwen read their spines, an unpleasant curling sensation rippling up her own.

"Robert's account books!" Charlotte announced.

"He doesn't keep everything on a computer?" Gwen asked, hoping she wasn't seeing what was right before her eyes.

"We're both computer illiterates," Charlotte announced.

Gwen remembered. Charlotte wrote her screenplays longhand before hiring a typist. Robert, for all his smarts, had a bookkeeper jot down every transaction in red or black ink.

It was one thing to proudly let a century of technical advances pass you by, another to steal corporate documents. Gwen rounded on her sister, unable to contain her anger any longer. "You stole these!"

"Robert's been hiding his financial data from me. I have a right to know."

"This isn't *All the President's Men!* You can't just break in—"

"It was at the house in Long Beach. I can take what's in my own house."

"I can't look at these."

"You're not looking, you're auditing."

"I most certainly am not."

Charlotte grabbed the sleeve of Gwen's hastily donned blouse, a Fury bent on vengeance. "I know you don't want to believe it, but I told you all along he was hiding something. This is it—from his office to the cedar closet. Is that suspicious or what?"

"Char, you question his motives when he passes you the toast."

"Look. I told you he'd try to swindle me, and here's the proof. I also told you Dave would be in on it."

Gwen stepped back involuntarily. "Don't even start."

Charlotte fumbled through the pile of ledgers. "Look how much has been deposited in Dave's account since Robert began managing it. Someone's getting paid off."

"For what?"

"For what do you think?" Dave asked, walking out of the master bedroom.

He'd left the shower dripping behind him. A soft plop-plop sounded under the towering peak of the living room as he walked toward them. His hair clung in spikes over his forehead. He'd ruffled the part on top to air dry. Now he slicked the sides with his hands, squeezing out droplets of water that raced down his clean-shaven cheek to the white towel around his neck. Except for cutoffs, the rest of him was skin, and Gwen knew every inch of it.

She looked guiltily at the pile of ledgers.

"Morning, Charlotte," Dave said.

Charlotte loyally threw her arm around her sister. "You won't succeed, either of you. We Stickerts stick together, and we've uncovered your plot!"

"Which one was that?"

"Dave, please don't tease." Gwen's voice was unusually flat. She wished she could force some levity into it, regain the teasing smile she'd found with him. Instead everything sounded like an accusation, like a woman reserving judgment. "You two weren't plotting against Charlotte, were you?"

"Do I have to answer that, counselor?" He shrugged, twisting the ends of the towel in each hand and answered his own question. "No, we haven't. Your sister's imagination is running wild again."

"You sound just like Robert when you say that," Charlotte declared.

He did, Gwen thought. But Dave and Rob were opposites; Robert never let anything go and Dave let everything go. Holding on meant caring and caring meant getting hurt. Better to pretend it didn't matter. Which he was doing right now.

She ached for him. She wanted to rush to him and throw her arms around his waist. The way Charlotte would. "They're nothing alike," Gwen insisted smoothly, turning to her sister.

"You're defending *him*?"

Someone had to. Left on his own, Dave would merely shrug and walk away, retreating as he had after his parent's divorce.

Momentarily stumped, Charlotte flew into action. Marching to the bedroom door, she surveyed the rumpled sheets Dave hadn't bothered to straighten. "You can't deny I saw it all coming."

True. But Gwen wouldn't cheapen it either. "We love each other, no matter how hard you find that to believe. It wasn't a plot."

Dave sauntered to Gwen's side. "Call it fate or the power of all these quartz crystals up here."

Gwen tensed. How could he joke when her head pounded and her nerves twisted into barbed wire? Hysteria, anger, arguments all rolled off his back—

—and landed smack on Gwen's shoulders. Caught in the middle as always. It was up to her to straighten things out. If only she could look at those books. Her fingertips strayed across their clammy surfaces, chilled from the auto air-conditioning Charlotte used full blast. "Dave, I can prove you weren't in on this."

"You need proof?" he asked.

"In an ideal world, no."

"Robert and I invested in a mutual fund together. Is that a crime?"

"If Robert is hiding assets, Charlotte has a right to know."

"That's between her and Robert."

"But I can help."

"If you want to take sides."

"Don't make me choose," Gwen pleaded.

He wiped a streak of water from the side of his neck. "You're free to do anything you want. You always have been, with me," he added. He squinted toward the loft. "I won't even hold you to the promise you made this morning."

"He didn't make you sign anything!" Charlotte hissed.

Gwen swatted her away, walking up to within inches of Dave's chest. She wanted to lay her hands there, just to touch him. "I promised to be yours."

He shrugged in his most infuriatingly indifferent manner, as if it didn't matter anyway. "Don't worry about it."

"I promised," she insisted, the lump in her throat almost choking her.

"And I thought we agreed a relationship comes first. Over winning, over being right. Over family."

But family had been around her all her life; Dave wouldn't promise her more than a day at a time.

"When Dad left, Charlotte and Mom and I only had each other to cling to."

"And you were the glue holding them together."

"It's a hard habit to break, taking care of everybody's crises."

"And when you get that responsibility at twelve, it's pretty heady, isn't it? That kind of power. Why else rush up here to save a marriage that isn't even yours?"

"I'm supporting my sister."

His jaw clenched, he purposely relaxed it, counting to make his point the way Robert would, a way Gwen might understand. "One: Your misplaced loyalty is destroying us; and Two: I don't see how it's helping them any."

Gwen angrily waved his fingers away from under her nose. "Don't you talk to me about loyalty, Dave King! Your freedom comes first, it always has. Loving one day at a time is not a commitment!" The words tumbled out so fast, the hand that flew to her mouth couldn't stem them—nor her gasp of surprise. "Dave, I'm sorry."

He stopped her apology with a shake of his head, a droplet of water landing on her cheek like a tear. "I told you I'd never care for anything so much, it'd destroy me to walk away. I'll prove it."

He climbed the ladder to the loft without looking back. Charlotte and Gwen listened to drawers being scraped out of the dresser, the slap of drawing pads piled one atop the other. In minutes his duffel thudded to the floor. He climbed halfway down, then jumped the rest. After several trips to the car he lashed the easel to the Camaro's ski rack and tossed in his finished drawings, rolled in cardboard tubes.

The car engine revved.

Gwen peered at the stained glass window beside the door. She wiped away the droplet of water on her cheek and found three more eager to join it. She licked their salty taste off her lips.

For a second she wanted to rant and rave, to wail to

the rafters above, to run after him, to beg. But that's what Charlotte would do. Gwen had to be calm, for everyone else's sake. She should have seen it coming. Dave met none of her requirements for a long-term commitment—except that she loved him more than she could bear to think right now.

Her sister touched her shoulders, hovering beside her like an overprotective mother. "Do you want anything to drink, hon?"

"Just let me get organized. I can handle this." Gwen could handle anything.

She pushed the On switch on her adding machine and listened to the tape scrape out the far side. She picked up a twelve-column pad, a mechanical pencil.

At the end of the drive, Dave burned rubber, spewing gravel and stripping gears. Gwen wrapped her arms across her middle and listened to his engine a mile down the mountain.

He had no right to make her choose. She had to work this out between Charlotte and Robert, prove with numbers that their suspicions were groundless. When she was done, she'd figure out what to do about Dave.

It wasn't over. It couldn't be.

If he loved her, he wouldn't walk away. Fights were messy, no matter what the rules. He'd drive around. He'd come back. If not, she knew where he lived. He had her number. There were family get-togethers.

The idea of seeing him twice a year tore into her like claws. She held her breath and leaned over the ledger until the pain passed. They'd work it out.

But first, she'd do what she came to do, settle this problem for Charlotte and Robert. She began by listing their assets.

By Sunday morning Gwen was barely aware of Charlotte cleaning away another plate of uneaten food. Adding-machine tape unrolled over the floor like a dockside streamer long after the ship has sailed. Figures and pencil markings littered her neat columns like ants at a picnic.

"Back ache?" Charlotte asked.

Everything ached, from the inside out. Her stomach knotted. Her heart hurt. Even her fingernails ached. "I'll be okay."

Gwen had checked and rechecked everything. A fairly accurate reading of Robert's legal practice lay before her. The records matched the financial statement he'd given Charlotte's attorney. There was no swindle. Gwen rubbed her eyes and breathed a sigh of relief. She wouldn't have to go to Dave with proof his brother lied.

Did that mean he won? Or did she? *You both lost,* a tiny voice said. She refused to listen. She'd done what she had to do, certainly he'd see that. With the audit complete, they'd put the feud behind them.

In fact, when she thought about it, when her mind wasn't reeling with lack of sleep, food, and too many numbers, she looked forward to getting their lives in order even more than Charlotte's.

A car slowed to a halt in the drive. She closed her eyes and prayed. She'd known Dave wouldn't just walk away.

The door opened.

Cool, collected, Robert strode to the dining room before saying hello. "Charlotte. Gwen."

Gwen glanced behind him. No Dave, just a yawning empty doorway. She swallowed her disappointment, then noticed the briefcase under his arm.

It took Charlotte a second longer. "My screenplay," she screeched.

"You were so eager to snatch my books, you left it at Long Beach." Swinging the brown leather like a man on his way to a bus stop, Robert ambled onto the deck, glanced around, and came back inside.

"Dave told you where we were," Charlotte cried accusingly.

"No he didn't," Gwen replied, jumping to her feet.

Robert paused in front of the fireplace. "You're

right, he didn't. He hasn't had much to say at all this weekend."

"How is he?" she asked.

Robert answered icily. "Cooped up in his apartment drawing night and day. That's what he always does when he's upset."

Gwen glanced up at the loft. He'd taken the sketches of her. He'd rolled her up in a hollow tube and gone. "But he's all right. I mean, he's okay."

"Nothing ever bothers Dave."

She hoped that wasn't true. She wanted to bother him, for him to hurt as much as she did. The idea of his being able to walk away from her so coldly and completely was inconceivable.

For once she understood what kept Charlotte and Robert together through all the pain—anything was better than having a gaping hole near her heart.

The snick of briefcase latches sounded in the silence. Robert extracted a handful of pages and proceeded to squirt them with the can of lighter fluid he'd picked up on the deck.

"Stop!" Charlotte shouted.

"I'm burning it."

"Gwen! Stop him!"

For some reason, Gwen's feet refused to move. Exhausted, she swayed, righting herself by holding on to the table.

Robert lit a match.

"No!" Charlotte's scream would've done the bride of Frankenstein proud.

For a second, that's exactly how Gwen saw them, a couple of spoiled, self-centered monsters tormenting each other. If anger was the only form of togetherness they had left, Gwen wanted no part of it. "Your problems are your own making."

Flipping the last ledger closed, she lined up her pencils, the memory of Dave's messy pastels taunting her. If only she'd told Charlotte to audit those books herself, or get another accountant. She'd spent a

lifetime evening out Charlotte's highs and lows, tran-
quilizing, placating, soothing her mother's woes. . . .

It was too late for regrets. All she had was here and
now, as Dave would say. But he wasn't here. And she
wanted him now. She owed him the day she'd promised him. And a lot more.

"Where are you going?" Charlotte demanded.

"I'm your sister, not your keeper. You two settle it."
Gwen lifted one ledger from the table and handed it
to Robert. "Burn these while you're at it. In the
courtroom you may be brilliant, Rob, but your books
are a mess."

"Don't you criticize my husband!"

Gwen stumbled into the bedroom and collapsed on
the bed. A bitter, rueful laugh hung in the air behind
her, mixing with the sharp tang of lighter fluid.

"Well?" Robert crouched beside the grating, his
knee cracking.

Charlotte knew the touch football game that had
caused his injury. The same way she knew the
precise amount of sleep he'd lost to make the circles
beneath his eyes so dark. She just didn't know what
to say next. "Well." She folded her arms, muumuu
swaying brightly.

"What'd she do to Dave?" Robert asked.

"She did nothing to him. Gwen couldn't—" She
lowered her voice. "You really think Gwen could
seduce her way out of a paper bag?"

"That's a cliché and a nonsensical image, but as a
matter of fact, I think your sister is very attractive. In
a muted sort of way."

Charlotte evened out her lipstick with a hurried
pressing of her lips. She swept a tightly curled black
ringlet across her mane of hair. "She's been hurt too."

"We all have."

She hugged her arms over her middle, kneading
them with ten blood-red nails. "Whose fault is that?"

"Everybody's."

She shook a finger at him. "If you told Dave to
sweet-talk her, I'll never forgive you."

"What else is new? You never forgive me anything."

"Me? Who's the one who refuses to let this fight die?"

"You're the one who audited my books."

"And you insisted on seizing the cottage."

"You wrote this screenplay."

"You tried to take Long Beach away."

Robert's laughter ended on a long sigh as he slicked back his hair with one hand. "We've had so much to fight about—"

"—what do we have to stay married for?" Charlotte's tremulous voice faltered.

Robert fiddled with his bow tie. Frustrated with the knot, he grabbed one end and untied it with a savage tug, then he flung it in the fireplace and snapped open his collar button. "We stay married, we fight, we do all of it because I won't let you go. Dammit, Charlotte, I told you the day we married I'm yours forever. For better or however worse we can make it."

Charlotte took one step forward, reaching tentatively for him. Robert closed the gap in two strides and dragged her into his arms. "It's all my fault."

"It's mine."

A storm of emotion enveloped them, Charlotte seizing his face in hers and covering him with kisses. He did the same, preferring to go directly to her mouth, that irritating, exasperating, volatile, luscious mouth.

Charlotte hiccuped through her tears and hugged him tight. "Let's not ever let it get that bad again."

"Never."

They paused in a long embrace until Charlotte gasped and held him at arm's length. "What do we do about Dave and Gwen?"

"You switch subjects faster than a lawyer with a guilty client, you know that?"

"Gwen calls me mercurial."

"As if that's a bad quality. I have to give her credit, though, if she caught that brother of mine."

"But we brought them together, we have to fix this."

"How? We aren't exactly experts on making up, Lotty."

She colored girlishly at his endearment. "We'll work on it. After we work on us." She led him to the lower level. Arm in arm they walked down the stairs, one step at a time.

"Bright, if not early," Gwen muttered to the receptionist as she hauled her textbooks to her desk. A stack of messages and projects greeted her. None from Dave. In three weeks, there'd been none at all.

He was in New York signing contracts, or so Robert had said when he and Charlotte had completed their second honeymoon and returned to L.A.

August 28 stared up from her desk calendar, ominously circled. It was the twenty-ninth; her CPA exam was over and done, and she could get on with her life. What there was of it. She wadded the daily page into a tight ball and banked it off the wall into the wastebasket.

"Two points," Candy said. The receptionist set down a cup of tea for Gwen.

"Two points, two days, two years." Two days for a CPA exam she'd spent two years fretting over. All that drive, all that effort, and it didn't seem half as important anymore. She heard Dave's voice. *You know it or you don't.*

She knew she'd passed. She also knew she loved him; it was the one sure thing in her life. But all the studying in the world hadn't helped her figure out when to see him again, what to say, how to apologize.

When her mother had learned she'd left Robert and Charlotte unsupervised at the cottage, she'd been accused of taking leave of her senses. "No, Mom," she'd murmured into the telephone, staring up at the crack in the ceiling, "I've taken leave of my heart."

In her office, she stared unseeing at the artwork on

the walls, wishing it had a little more color, more splashes of red and deep purples. More life.

"Your sister on Line One," Candy said, nodding toward the blinking pink light.

She hung up in five minutes. Dinner was the least Charlotte could do for her.

"You set me up."

"Gwen, don't get upset."

Gwen turned her head slowly toward her sister. "Do I ever?" Maybe it was high time she started. She began by raising her voice. "You never said Dave would be here."

"Rob invited him. How could I say no? We don't fight anymore."

"So it's the four of us for dinner. How cozy." Indulging in a little sarcasm actually felt good.

"It had to be tonight," Charlotte explained. "I wanted to give you the dress."

The dress was a hand-me-down but a glittering one. Charlotte had enticed Gwen into the bedroom and got her to try it on just in time for Dave to ring the doorbell.

"Red looks great on redheads."

"The way it slides off makes me look like a barber-shop pole." Gwen tugged it up where it slouched off her shoulder. The thing only had one sleeve.

"You look wonderful. I wish I had your shape."

"And I wish I had your gall," Gwen retorted.

Dave's voice resounded from the front hallway, bouncing off all the faux marble Charlotte had installed. She smiled beseechingly at her sister. "Be nice to him."

A smidgen of satisfaction played behind Gwen's smile; she'd never been the volcano everyone tiptoed around before. "I'll try."

But the tough facade crumbled as Charlotte led her down the hallway. He sounded good. Happy. His laugh made her skin shimmer like the red sequins she wore; the tiny hairs on her arms sprang up. She'd wanted to see him for a month.

She hadn't wanted to see him looking like hell. The smile vanished from her eyes the moment she saw him.

His did the same. "Gwen."

"Dave. So much for the dress," she muttered out the side of her mouth, disengaging her elbow from Charlotte's grasp. "I could've worn knee socks for all the good this did."

Dave's brows rose. "You wore that for me?"

"Yes, no," Gwen and Charlotte replied simultaneously. They traded looks.

Dave raked a hand through his tussled hair and smiled a pained smile in the direction of the floor. "Shall we try that again?"

"No, she didn't," Charlotte insisted.

"Yes, I did," Gwen replied, lying with aplomb. "Just call me Miss Firecracker." She spread wide her arms and twirled.

Good Lord, she'd never felt so uncomfortable around Dave. Because he made her laugh, she thought, dispelling the tension she'd carried around so long.

Anyone with a heart would do the same for him. He acknowledged her fashion show as if smiling hurt his face. The parentheses around his mouth had deepened, she suspected more from grim concentration than laughter. His hair looked as if it hadn't seen a comb since the first issue of *Superman*, and he didn't seem to know what to do with his hands.

"Got a beer, Rob?" he asked.

"Got a case. Come on in."

Four abreast, they walked into the living room, Rob to the far right, Charlotte to the left, and Dave and Gwen firmly in between. The married couple quickly excused themselves to the kitchen.

"I'll get you a bottle," Robert offered.

"I'll get you a glass," Charlotte chimed.

"He doesn't need a glass," Robert stated.

"He does," Charlotte hissed, giving her husband a subtle shove from behind.

Dave smiled stiffly at Gwen. "Thought they were going to chain our ankles together to keep us from bolting. Obviously you knew about this." He nodded at the dress.

She didn't waste time defending herself. "It's good to see you." Good to really look at him after all this time. Gangly traces of youth still animated his movements, but the regrets of an older man shadowed his eyes—regrets she'd put there.

"You're looking sharp."

"As a thumbtack," she replied brightly. "Charlotte loaned it to me." She lifted the hem to reveal her bare feet. "Not really my style. I feel like a sardine slathered in jam."

He blinked. "I don't think I could paint that picture if you paid me."

"I'd pose for free."

They contemplated each other a long minute.

"What was that all about, Gwen?"

He meant the argument at the cottage. For a moment hope sprang in her. If they could communicate so well in shorthand, maybe they weren't as far apart as she feared. "I've been asking myself the same question for a month."

"Knowing you, you've probably worked out all the answers."

She shook her head. "Didn't know where to begin. We need to do that together."

Charlotte scooted in with a tray of bottles. "Dinner will be a little late."

"Caterer cancel?"

Charlotte jangled her bracelets at Dave with a scolding shake of her finger. "I've taken up cooking. You'll have to try it."

"Dave's a great cook," Gwen said, catching his piercing gaze, knowing he, too, recalled all those meals at the cottage. Snacks on the deck, in the hammock, breakfasts in bed . . .

"I meant he should try eating. He's so skinny."

He had lost weight. The comment gave Gwen an excuse to look him up and down.

He spread his arms and turned slowly around for her inspection. "The hungry artist himself. Ready when you are."

Eleven

Ready when you are. Gwen was ready to scream. Before taking lessons in clothes sense from her sister, she should have learned a thing or two on how to hit the ceiling, how to blow one's top, how to grab a man by the lapels and *make* him talk.

Instead, she took her seat politely beside Charlotte. Charlotte immediately popped up and joined Rob on the opposite sofa, displacing Dave with the words, "I want to snuggle next to my sweetie."

"No prob," Dave replied wryly. "I always enjoyed musical chairs."

"Okay, you two. You know something's up," Charlotte began.

"Looks like me," Dave quipped.

"Sit beside Gwen," Robert ordered.

He hitched his slacks and did as he was told.

"You two look as if you've been called to the principal's office." Robert laughed.

"Seriously," Charlotte cooed. "We wanted you both here so we could thank you for reuniting us."

Gwen demurred, Dave did likewise.

"Our troubles really were half my fault," Rob said to his brother. "You pointed it out, but I wouldn't listen."

"Half my fault, too, honey," Charlotte added. "I was such a shrew!"

"So Kate and Petruchio are happy at last. Can we eat now?"

"Dave!" Gwen scolded, trying to keep the laughter out of her voice. She'd been thinking the same thing. "We really didn't do any more than sit ringside."

"The lady's right."

"Thanks, Dave."

"Anytime," he said quietly, hooking a finger under his collar.

Gwen looked at the hands clasped in her lap.

"In return," Charlotte continued with forced enthusiasm, "we simply had to do something for you."

"Don't think we were completely blind to what transpired between you two," Rob said with a wink.

"Here!" Charlotte reached behind a sofa cushion and dramatically drew out two rolled pieces of paper tied with ribbons. "These saved our marriage, and we think they'll help you over the rough spots."

A full-load grader couldn't even out their rough spots, Gwen thought despairingly, taking the paper in her hand.

"Your diplomas in marriage counseling." Robert chuckled.

Gwen and Dave unrolled them simultaneously. Dave lifted his glass to his lips, then lowered it slowly as he scanned the page.

"*Fighting Fair*," Gwen croaked. "Ten Rules for Resolving Conflict in a Marriage."

"On parchment no less."

She could have laughed. She almost wept. She worked up the nerve to glance at Dave. His mouth was drawn in a tight line as his eyes flickered back and forth. He read every word.

She cleared her throat when she saw he'd finished. "Not a bad idea, huh?"

Charlotte covered Dave's silence. "It was just the breakthrough we needed to see what we'd been doing wrong."

"Agreed," Robert replied.

Dave folded the paper into smaller and smaller squares, finally stuffing it in the inside pocket of his sport coat. "The biggest lesson of all should be not interfering in other people's problems." He stood. "I propose a toast to lists."

Gwen lifted her glass of ginger ale. "I'll drink to that."

"I thought you would."

On second thought, she wouldn't. Not when the ginger ale caught in her throat like acid.

"You know," Dave said to her, "if they'd seen this list that first night, we'd have gotten out of there in a week."

And we'd have never fallen in love. Gwen completed the unspoken thought, crumpling the paper in her hands. "I need a walk."

The shady side of the in-ground pool offered little respite from the ninety-degree day. Distance made Charlotte and Robert's scolding nothing but an angry buzzing behind her.

"How could you, David?" Gwen heard Charlotte say.

"We're only trying to help, buddy."

She couldn't decipher his curt reply.

Gwen sank to the stone bench, shielding her eyes from the glare off the water. When she uncovered them, a pair of scuffed deck shoes stood patiently in her line of view. Bony feet, no socks. "Hi, Dave."

"Did you give her this?" He tapped his coat pocket.

"She must have discovered it for herself." She waved a hand at the landscaped setting. "Like Dorothy in Oz finding happiness in her own backyard. I'm surprised you didn't fold it into an origami swan or dragon."

"Not feeling that creative lately."

She squinted into the sun beyond his shoulder. "You don't look it, either." Khaki slacks and a plain cotton shirt buttoned to the throat didn't suit the

Dave she knew. The sport coat was very suave. Very suave wasn't Dave.

He fingered a bunch of olives dangling over her head. She heard the snap of a twig. Sitting on the edge of the bench, he plucked leaves off it one by one. "Sorry I was abrupt in there. I didn't mean it exactly the way it came out."

"Want to try again?" She wished he would read all the same meanings into that line that she did. "I thought it was crystal clear."

"Other people's affairs are dangerous if you let them affect your own."

"I shouldn't have looked at the books, I know."

"It's over and done."

It isn't, she wanted to cry. She watched him pare the last leaves away before she snatched the twig out of his hand. "Here." She handed it back.

"What's that for?"

She nudged him with her elbow. "I'm offering you an olive branch. Boy, you've gotten slow."

He ran a hand over his mouth as if wiping away a smile, then he kneaded the tension in his neck. "Why the kidding around? You usually get right to the point."

"It's the least I can do. Go ahead, take the entire tree. Make fun of this fire-hydrant dress. Anything. Just don't tell me you wished it never happened." *And please don't look so wounded.*

"We lived it like we lived it, and I wouldn't have missed it for the world," he concluded. "Happy?"

"Ecstatic."

"We did have fun," he finally admitted, reaching back for another twig.

For a heart-jarring second she thought he was reaching for her. "We had more than that."

He shrugged. "You needed laughs."

"I needed you."

"You needed the vacation. *Amazon Women Warriors* is finished and fantastic." He didn't mention how much of that he owed to her influence. "They raved about it at the publishers'."

"Don't derail the discussion."

"Didn't know we were working from an agenda. Are we going to haggle over this until it's settled?" he asked.

"Maybe not here and now, but we could work it out. One day at a time. I promised you that."

"I won't hold you to it."

"Hold me! Make us work this out!"

If he heard her strained command, it didn't show. "You can't force people to love you anymore than you can make them stay if they want to go," he said simply.

"Did I ever force you?"

"No, but you made your choice. How could I stay at the cottage after watching you relegate us to second in line?"

Gwen fidgeted on the bench, tightly clasping her hands. "I thought I could have it both ways. I planned on getting to us after I helped them."

"Taking me for granted already." He laughed humorlessly.

"I was wrong."

He gripped her hand where she touched his arm, kissing her palm in a hurried, clumsy way, never meeting her brimming eyes. Then he released her. "I thought I was tired of easy. But I don't know if I can deal with this, Gwen. It's too much, too deep."

Like the ten-foot marker at the end of the pool, he was in over his head. Rising, he paced to the edge where turquoise tiles formed a dolphin's tail. Crouching, he dragged his hand through the smooth surface, scaring up ripples.

"Please try," she pleaded softly. "I'm asking, not insisting. No chains. No ties." A tentative smile crooked her lips as she joined him, touching his naked collar button, a blatant effort to tease a smile out of his haggard face. "I bet you don't even own a tie."

Come to think of it, he didn't. That's what he got for loving an intelligent woman, he thought, she saw right through him. He winced at the idea of what she might see.

He needed space.

She gave it to him. Alone at the other end of the pool, he realized she hadn't chased after him when he'd walked out, hadn't so much as called. Why was he so scared of a clinging woman dragging him down? He wasn't his father.

And she wasn't the furious, sword-wielding Beli-Zar. Days after driving back from Arrowhead, steeped in his work, he'd discovered Beli-Zar's counterpart, a wise woman whom the warrior maiden sought for advice. She had Gwen's face, her body, her sweet sensible spirit. For the next three weeks he'd lived with both women—the one who slew her dragons and the one who figured out how life proceeded when the dragons were gone. Real life.

Gwen was that heroine, and he'd failed her. Hard as it was to face, the fact stared back at him like his reflection in the pool. Then she came into view in the water like a vision, glancing over his shoulder.

Elbows resting on his knees as he crouched at the water's edge, Dave squinted at her reflection.

"If this is hard for you, it's just as hard for me," Gwen said. "I've never been a fighter either; I'm the one who referees."

"It's a lot safer standing on the sidelines blowing a whistle, offering advice and solutions. Easier than getting in the game, Gwen."

"But what happens when it stops being a game? When you have to get serious?"

"When a relationship's secure, people can kid themselves, laugh at their faults. It's when things get serious that you know it's falling apart."

She laughed, the sound choking in her throat when she realized he meant what he'd said. "It doesn't have to. But you can't play at love either, keeping it all on the surface, never letting it get more than skin-deep."

"You saying I didn't love you?"

"I'm saying it was my skin. If you won't talk to me, how do I know this wasn't about sex? Or maybe it was a lark. The pillow fights and the tickling and the private jokes—getting your uptight old-maid sister-in-law in bed—"

Rising abruptly, Dave uttered a curse as ugly as her insinuations and dashed his glass against the serene surface of the pool. The water shattered, splinters of splashing light and jagged airborne rainbows hovered over the pool as their reflections shuddered and dissolved.

Gwen recoiled, gripping the skirt of her dress.

"If you believe that, there's nothing I can say." Dave muttered another expletive, shooting a black look at his brother and Charlotte standing behind the patio doors. They ducked behind a curtain. "Maybe they can tell us how to solve this. They're the experts." He turned on his heel and headed for the drive.

Gwen raised her voice, hurling the words at his back. "You wanted this to be easy? Then take the easy way out. Run away."

He stopped, squaring his spine as if a blade had pierced it. "You think this is easy?"

The rasped words tore at her heart. She fought to keep herself from running after him, from grasping his arms in her hands and shaking him. It would be like shaking a tree rooted to the spot—and it would be too much like what Charlotte would do. They had to find their own answers.

And if, in the end, they simply didn't work as a couple, they'd have to face the fact and stop hurting each other.

"I didn't mean that," she said unsteadily, "what I just said. We're not very good at fighting, are we?"

"You'll get no argument here."

"I don't want one."

"Neither do I." He held up his hand, stopping her

next statement. "Gwen, don't start building a case one carefully reasoned argument at a time, all right? That isn't the way I deal with stuff like this."

"How do you deal with it?"

"I don't." It was news to him, although he should have seen it coming a long time ago.

She hugged herself, and he became aware of how bare her one shoulder was, sensing the warm breath of air wafting across it. And the cold gulf that remained between them. "Why didn't you tell me you minded the one-day-at-a-time thing?"

"Until you began waving loyalty at me, I didn't realize I did. I repress anger, I don't express it."

"I *was* committed to you, Gwen. Every day. What more did you want?"

"All of it. My father walked out on us every time voices were raised. I can't tiptoe around other people's tempers all my life. I need to know we can disagree and you'll still be there."

"If staying is up to me, I'll stay. But I can't be chained, Gwen. That's hell, not love."

She stared at the grass. At the cottage, she'd looked at the books rather than at him, as if her feelings would overwhelm her common sense, her resolve crumbling like her mother's had every time her father had returned.

"This is us, not them," she said, struggling to control her tears. "We seem to be right back where we started, a million miles apart."

She gripped the edge of her dress and yanked it up, gathering the hem in one hand. She had to pass him to reach the driveway. Her hand shook too hard to touch him again. "I'm getting out of here before I make a total fool of myself."

She stalked around the pool toward the drive.

Dave watched her walk away, her reflection broken as she trod through a puddle by the diving board. Damp footprints traced her path across the stones. *This way,* they seemed to say.

He remained where he was.

His Amazon Queen would have strode, leapt, stalked. Gwen picked her way carefully over the prickly grass. She didn't go barefoot often, not his Gwen.

If she ever takes it up, you won't be the one walking with her. The insight flickered through him like light from his beer glass revolving at the bottom of the pool.

He tormented himself with the image, picturing the safe, sane man she'd meet in an office someday, a climate-controlled building lit with fluorescent tubes— not a stained glass window in sight. A man who wouldn't tickle her without express permission, who wouldn't make her wrinkle up her nose at bad puns or serious fashion mistakes like Hawaiian shirts.

Comic books would not be their bedtime reading.

Dave would give them matching adding machines for their wedding and play the good sport at the reception. This time he'd know better than to kiss her.

That was how the whole thing had started. Not with them a million miles apart, but body to body, kissing on a dance floor.

"Where's she going?" Robert asked, scurrying over to join him beside the pool.

Once upon a time Dave had wanted to make her happy. All he had to show for it now were two miserable people. And his freedom. "What good does it do?" he asked no one in particular, watching Gwen turn as she got into her car.

She spotted him and his brother standing shoulder to shoulder. "Rob said your work was going well," she called. She opened her mouth to say more, couldn't, and got in.

Robert trotted back to the house in answer to Charlotte's frantic hand signals. They bowed their heads in hushed consultation.

Dave shoved his fists into his pockets. *Stop her, you idiot. Do something.* Maybe the words were Charlotte's urgent promptings from the patio doorway. Maybe they came from his heart. Either way, his feet began to move.

Turning the key, Gwen started the car and wiped her eyes. After loudly blowing her nose, she turned the key again. The car produced a hideous grinding noise. She smiled sheepishly at Dave as he paused on the edge of the driveway. A tear leaked out when he came no further.

"Rob mentioned the gallery," she said, dabbing a crushed tissue against a puffy pink nose. As if Robert explained everything.

Did he mention how Dave had lost all interest in his first private showing? How he'd tried submersing himself in the battles and carnage, only to return time and again to reason and common sense?

Good versus evil didn't capture Dave's attention the way it once had. The most difficult battle was the kind that had to be resolved to both parties' satisfaction, the kind where your opponent loved you when all was said and done. Would always love you.

Only the stuttering Ragnar, sensitive Viking Thane, had come close to expressing the quandary on paper. *And your sketches of Gwen,* a quiet voice reminded him. Those sketches showed how much he needed her. She was part of him. He wouldn't be destroyed if she left—he'd survive. But he'd be lessened.

What was commitment if not the ultimate freedom? The freedom to make promises. A real man had the guts to stand behind them.

She put the car in gear and turned the key again.

Dave cringed at the grating noise. "Anyone with that touch ought to drive an automatic," he called.

She laughed, bit her lip, and let out the clutch. Gravel crunched beneath her tires as she pulled slowly down the drive.

He considered offering her a ride home. The woman wasn't in any condition to drive. What if she pulled into traffic without looking, got sideswiped or forced off the road, had a flat tire on the freeway?

A host of dire possibilities assailed him. A veritable

list of what could go wrong on the L.A. freeways. He couldn't let her go.

Dave raced down the curved drive, vaulting the hedges in one bound, and landed smack on the gardener. He hit the ground and rolled.

Gwen hit the brakes, screeching to a halt half in and half out of the drive. "What are you doing?"

"Sorry, Mr. Sing!" he called over his shoulder after making sure the old man was okay. He trotted up to her car. Shrugging his sport coat back into place, he leaned suavely on the driver's-side door, as if hurdling gardeners was an everyday occurrence.

Gwen choked back a laugh that might have emerged as a sob. Grass stained his sleeves. Clipped pieces of hedge sprouted in his hair. She hurriedly wiped her tears away, hopelessly smudging her glasses from the inside.

"Hey babe," he said with a leer, "what say you come up to my place and see my sketches?" He waggled his brows.

Her heart caught in her throat. For a moment she'd thought he was about to declare his feelings. But nothing, and no one, ever really changed. Dave was back to playing games. Her emotions ricocheted from resignation to a sweet fond indulgence that was too much like a tender form of love. "No thanks, Casanova."

"I've got some tasteful nudes."

"Thanks, I've seen the model—not always on her better days."

"This was one of her best," he said, his voice low and a trifle hoarse.

Gwen memorized his eyes, the thick straw-color hair. Yes, that had been one of her very best days. Like all her days with Dave. And all their nights.

She curled her fingers around the steering wheel until they turned white. She wanted him playful, she wanted him serious, she wanted him period. But she'd hurt them both, and she'd never, ever wanted that.

They were wrong for each other. She should have known better. She had once. Before he'd charmed her and made her laugh, made her forget caution and goals and guarantees.

"I can't," she said, staring through her streaked windshield.

If only she'd had some time to prepare her arguments, some time to think. But Charlotte had arranged for him to show up at the end of that hallway, and Gwen had ruined her only chance to win him back. She'd promised herself once it wouldn't end with demands, tearful apologies, scenes. It wouldn't.

"I really ought to go." She reassembled her dignity and shifted in her seat. "Sorry."

"Sure thing." He cuffed her door with the side of his fist to speed her on her way. "Come see 'em before the gallery showing."

"Maybe I will. Good-bye."

Like a twenty-four-hour time-release capsule, the meaning of his words hit her the next evening after she'd ripped open the notification announcing she'd passed her exam. "A gallery showing! Of *my* nudes!"

Pow! as one of Dave's panels would say.

Just what a brand new CPA needed, to be put on display before the public wearing nothing but a pillow!

The gate of the Malibu estate was wide open. Gwen signaled and turned in. Although Dave merely rented the apartment over the garage, the very idea of his living beside such an extravagant, sumptuous, rather garish house, impressed her. In a curious way, it pleased her.

It suited him. Turrets of cedar and bleached wood rose up between the entrance and the blue-green expanse of the Pacific. Tinted glass reflected the glinting golden sand, helping the house blend in with its surroundings.

As much as a house with a six-car garage can blend in with anything, Gwen thought. She took a deep breath and reviewed her arguments.

She had a dozen reasons why Dave couldn't show those pictures. And not a one covered the beefy security guard running toward her shouting something in Spanish. A rottweiler strained beside him on a very short leash as he slapped the hood of her car.

"Hey lady, no sightseers."

She gazed sheepishly into his reflecting sunglasses. "Excuse me?"

"Private property."

She cranked down the window, uttering a terrified squeak as the dog put its giant paws on her door and sniffed. "I'm not here to see MegaDeath or Guns n' Roses—"

"Breaking and Entering." He named the heavy-metal group that owned the house. "They're on tour."

"Wonderful." She smiled. "But I'm not here for breaking or entering." He didn't seem to get the joke. She adjusted her own glasses by looking into his. The dog drooled on the rust spots. "I'm here to see the man who lives over the garage. David King."

The guard grunted in an almost civilized manner and waved her on.

She parked and inhaled that peculiarly Californian scent of sun-soaked cement and salty air. Heat practically rose from the drive in wavy lines. Gwen smiled as she thought of Dave drawing them, then swallowed hard.

They were finished. She'd seen to that. No matter how long or how much she loved him, she'd only hurt him by insisting they stay together. One wanted commitment, the other freedom.

"Opposites in every way," she murmured.

Pulling herself together, she followed the unassuming wooden staircase up the outside of the garage to the second story. A deck on the ocean side ran along the front of the apartment. Beach and water and setting sun combined in bands of heart-stopping color. It wasn't hard to see where Dave got his inspiration.

"Hi." He stood below her on the sand, smiling up.

Her knees unlocked and started shaking. She was only there about the sketches. She had an agenda and she'd stick to it. The way she should have a month ago, her conscience prodded. A lifetime and a love affair ago.

She'd broken every rule she'd ever set. Sensible rules, created after much deep thought and deliberation. Similar ambitions, compatible goals, appropriate backgrounds, all tossed out the window because a lanky man's kisses made her blood heat in shimmery wavy lines, and words like *Whammo* and *Shazam* popped into her head whenever he smiled.

Oh Dave, why didn't we work? she thought with a pang.

Twelve

Nevertheless, he seemed inexplicably happy to see her.

She tried not to resent it. The young recovered fast.

As if to add to her irritation, the words "Don't worry, be happy" floated out of a tape deck beside him.

"I'm here about the sketches," she announced firmly.

Dave contentedly basted himself with more sunscreen, slathering it across a lean muscled chest. He looked sexy and scrumptious. Never mind that her whole life was at stake, not to mention her career and the ridicule of the general public.

"You look as if you're about to run away," he observed.

If he displayed those drawings, queues of total strangers would be critiquing her thighs. Stronger women had been known to quail at the prospect. "I had a run-in with that fire-breathing dog."

"Cerberus? He's all right as hellhounds go. Louie should have him under control."

"I don't know if 'should' is good enough." It would have to do. Lord knows, she'd been living by shoulds all her life.

She followed Dave's pointed finger to a white metal staircase and descended to the sand. "A movie star would love making an entrance like this," she said, clutching the handrail and hoping she didn't do something typically klutzy like tumble all the way to his feet. Or into his arms.

"Want to walk?" he asked.

"I came to talk."

"Then don't argue. You should walk barefoot more often." He'd been promising himself he'd encourage her to do just that. In fact, he'd planned everything, figuring it'd take about a day for her to show up. Gwen would think things over first, then drop by correctly claiming she was on her way home from work.

But she'd surprised him in subtle and indefinable ways. Her work clothes were softer than he'd expected. He'd envisioned her in two-piece suits with high-collared white blouses. Instead she wore a loose-sleeve silk T-shirt that rested lightly on her breasts, her skirt a billowing print. She was rich blues and sea greens and soft red hair. Sweeping it back off her face, she'd anchored a handful of fine hair to her crown with a hand-painted comb. He liked it.

He also liked the deliberate way she balanced herself while removing her shoes. Sensible Gwen.

"How far were you planning on walking?" she asked.

"Who plans?"

She gave him a dry look and set her sandals neatly on the bottom stair, marching after him across the sand as he backed toward the water. "If this was any hotter, it'd be glass," she shrieked. "Ooh, ah, eek."

"Nicely conjugated. Is this a conjugal visit?"

"Ha ha." She tripped another ten paces.

"If you go faster, you'll get done quicker."

"Breathtaking logic, but I can't. Who knows what's buried in here? Bottle tops, stones, fish skeletons, crustaceans of all kinds—"

"Listing the hazards?"

The greatest hazard of all descended on her, sweeping her into his arms and carrying her toward the surf.

"Don't!" she squealed, grasping his neck in a half nelson as the waves sloshed around his calves.

He gargled an unintelligible reply.

"Don't drop me!"

"Stop choking. I'd never!"

"Oh no?"

He paused, thinking, then grinned mischievously. He quickly found himself gasping as she blocked off his air passages once more. "Okay," he admitted with a wheeze, "it did occur to me, but only after you brought it up. I was saving you from the sand."

"Right. Like Delilah saved Samson from a lifetime of cream rinse."

"You know me too well, woman."

She only wished it were true. As he set her down, Gwen gathered her filmy skirt around her knees and felt the undertow drag at them. A large wave crashed around her legs.

"Tide's coming in. You might want to lift that a little higher." Dave traced a finger up her thigh, drawing a bead of moisture upward.

It almost sizzled. "You'd like that."

"You know what I like," he murmured.

She knew what he loved—his freedom more than her. She'd come for a reason, not to fall in love with the man all over again. "Dave, you can't show those pictures."

"I have a one-man show coming up."

She got his attention off her thighs and back to her face, which she hoped was suitably stern and reproving. "This woman isn't going to be part of it."

"No? I didn't get a gallery showing based on Beli-Zar. They want my serious work."

He'd never been more serious. Luring Gwen there had worked perfectly; after that all his plans fell apart. Waiting for instinct to tell him what to do now was sheer hell. "Come on inside and we'll talk about it." He offered to carry her back across the burning sand.

She took a minute to consider, as if weighing the difference between burned soles and broken hearts.

"Last one in slathers sun lotion on the other," he called over his shoulder. Making it a game, he raced toward the house, puffs of sand scooting from his heels.

Gwen scampered after, panting by the time they reached the bottom of the stairs. "Wait a minute. If you win, I put lotion on you, and if I win, you put lotion on me. Why do I get the feeling you win either way?"

He grinned rakishly. "We both win. I thought that was the point."

"You're being wise again."

Dave leaned in the doorway and let a long silent look answer that. "Coming?"

She brushed by him. He made sure of that. Rubbing her feet on the entry rug, Gwen refused to set foot inside until she'd got the sand out from between each toe.

The room was long and narrow, a wall of windows opposite a wall of white. Originals of his comic book covers alternated with surprisingly subtle watercolors and pen-and-ink studies. Beaches, villains, and birds rivaled each other for space, inhabiting worlds linked by color and motion.

"The watercolors are yours too?" she asked.

He nodded, waiting. He knew she had worked out what to say, how to say it, when to pause and give him an opening. He just didn't know how to take it. "Something to drink?"

"Lemonade?"

"I'll look."

Gwen walked the length of the room and deliberately studied the pictures one by one, beginning in the far corner. Superheroes of every shape and size vied with urban landscapes purpled by night. Yellow slashes of neon underlined their crowded loneliness. The comic book slant gave every picture a freshness and immediacy she hadn't seen in a host of gallery shows.

When she reached his end of the room, Dave handed her a glass of lemonade across the counter that formed the kitchen.

"Your work will be a smash, Dave."

"Thanks. I think my recent things are the best. I made a breakthrough, and you were part of that." He tipped his glass her way. "Thanks again."

She sipped her lemonade. "You're the one who deserves the thanks. I passed my test, did I tell you?"

"Fantastic." He came around the counter, slipped a hand around her waist, and gave her a chaste kiss. "Congratulations, Gwen. I knew you'd do it."

Gwen. Not babe, or hon, or love. Not even Charlotte's favorite, sweetie. Did that mean it was over for him too? Gwen knew she shouldn't feel weepy; she'd declared it finished herself. It was, all except the part about loving him.

"It wasn't bad, the exam," she said, forcing some lightness into her voice. "Except, when I went in, I sat down, opened my briefcase to get out my calculator, and one of your comic books fell out."

"Which one?"

She shrugged. "I was too busy stuffing it back inside to notice."

He made a tsking noise.

"That's exactly what the man across from me said!" They laughed.

"I told him I knew the artist and that you'd just won three Shazam awards."

"I'll bet he was impressed."

Gwen laughed and said no more.

She really shouldn't be so relaxed, shouldn't be teasing him, shouldn't be pondering socially acceptable ways of wangling an invitation to stay to dinner. She should state her business and leave.

As soon as she memorized where he lived, how he looked.

She faced the room, inhaling deeply of the ocean breeze. She contemplated the bleached wooden floors, the soft chairs covered in cottons, two-tones of off-white stripes. With the sun streaming in, the white room should have been blinding. It was comfortable, clean, and spacious. Easy to feel at home in. "Your apartment is gorgeous."

"Not a beer can in sight and all the dirty clothes safely stashed."

"I wasn't being condescending."

"Let me show you the rest of the pieces for the exhibit and you can compliment me some more. It's a treat to be praised by someone over fourteen, in words other than 'neat,' 'awesome,' or 'chillin.'"

He strode down a hallway to a workroom with a drafting table. Beneath high-intensity track lights, stacks of matted illustrations leaned against every wall. After oohing and ahing over the energy and subtlety in his work, Gwen followed him toward the bedroom when he held out the promise of more.

"Got pictures everywhere you look," he said, sliding a ladder-back chair out of the way with one foot, hoisting up two more pictures from the closet.

They could have been trolls for all she noticed. She stared at the space above his head.

The sketch of her curled and sleeping in his shirt was mounted over the bed. Matted and framed, it measured at least four feet by four feet. It was imposing. And intimate. It spoke of loneliness and love, thoughtfulness, passion. On a gallery wall it would command attention, even a kind of reverence. Over the bed, it took on an unmistakable air of erotica that made her skin flush.

All the public would see was a woman modestly clad in a shirt that scrupulously covered every erogenous zone. And yet, the slashing strokes of charcoal, the passionate detailing and sinuous lines made even the bony mound of her ankle seem sexy, cherished.

The question of her posing would inevitably arise. If she denied it, claimed he'd imagined the whole thing, people would undoubtedly reply, "He must have loved you very much to imagine this."

That's the conclusion she drew. Her eyes met his. He watched her as intently as he had when he'd done the sketch. She turned away.

And came face-to-face with the other nude.

"I call it *The Pillow Sketch*," he offered.

He might call it that. *She'd* call it wantonness incarnate. Nothing immodest showed. And yet the pillow was clearly the only thing the woman wore. Her thighs were rounded and malleable, the flesh softly tinted with pastels that fairly shouted a close and careful examination beforehand. He'd even caught a scattering of freckles just above her breasts.

Picturing it in a gallery was unthinkable. Picturing it in his room was worse, fixed to the wall he looked at as he lay in bed. The woman gazed back, knees slightly raised, hands flattening the pillow, pressing breasts unseen, her warm eyes steady and direct, unashamed, filled with their own dancing, daring magic.

"You can't show these." Her voice eddied out on a strangled breath. "Not in a gallery. If even one client saw them—"

"You might get some interesting propositions."

"I'm not interested in propositions." Proposals maybe, but not propositions. "It'd besmirch my reputation."

"Anybody smirches you, you call me."

"I hate it when I'm trying to be serious and you make me laugh!"

"I try not to. I've tried being everything you want me to be, short of wearing a tie."

"See? Even now you're joking."

"I'm an artist, I exhibit my work. You want me to change?"

"That's a loaded question and you know it."

"So point and shoot."

"No, I don't want you to change!" She rubbed the line between her brows, consciously lowering her voice. "What were we arguing about anyway?"

"You with no clothes on."

"*That* wasn't the point."

"Too bad. It's one of my favorite subjects." And it had worked for them before. That's what he'd realized yesterday. They were opposites in so many ways, and yet, whenever he touched her, they meshed perfectly. "If we're going to argue about these sketches—"

"We are."

"Then we ought to follow the rules."

"What rules?"

"How to fight fair." As if she could ever forget, his tone implied.

He pulled an inch-square piece of paper from the sport coat draped over the ladder-back chair. Then he led her to the bed and urged her to sit beside him.

She wriggled a good foot away, knees together, feet bare, toes tensely curled. She folded her hands on what would have to do for a lap. "What about them?"

"Remember the one about touching the other person when you argue?"

"Those are for lovers," she said, slanting a cautious glance his way.

"And what are we?"

She looked into his eyes, her gaze falling for a moment to his lips.

Before she could object, he skimmed them over her temple, feeling her lashes flutter shut, brushing his cheek like a sprite's wings. "This is where we came in." But sprites, fairies, and nymphs didn't radiate heat; their hearts didn't pound and their cheeks didn't blush. Only a woman's did that.

He cupped her jaw in his palm and aligned her mouth with his. "If we ever argue again, hold on to me."

"Are we arguing?" she asked, a delicate tremor in her voice.

"Just don't let go of me, Gwen, not yet."

He tugged the blouse off her shoulder, the one that had been bared to him the day before, the one he'd longed to kiss. He found the dip of her collarbone, the perfume behind her ear, the soft, heated expanse of her chest, and the giving fullness of her breasts, their sweet weight betrayed by the tight peaks of her nipples.

She moaned and pulled his head away from her, using the motion to run her hands through his hair once more. "Sex won't solve anything, Dave."

"You said it wouldn't start anything either. We built a relationship on expressing things physically."

"And it disappeared like a castle in the sand the first time we had an argument. I love you, but I can't go on loving you, not if you're capable of walking out every time we fight. Throw things, yell, be like Charlotte; I can handle that."

"I learned young not to let it get to me."

"Well, it got you. And it got to me." She felt the sharp scrape of stubble in her palm, the firm line of his cheekbone. "Anybody with eyes can see that."

"Do I look that bad?"

"Worse. Do I have to become a Beli-Zar, winning arguments with sword power?"

"Those brass cups are a bit kinky, but now that you mention it—"

"Dave."

"Yes, ma'am."

"We need to face this seriously."

"I agree. Because Rule Three says we can't go to bed until it's resolved."

"Is that what we're doing?"

"Touch me like you don't mean it, Gwen. Try to lie to me now."

"I never lied to you." The fervor of her words brooked no contradictions. And yet—

"You said we'd never make it," he muttered harshly, his mouth on her throat, her ear. "We were too different."

"We are."

"Not here. Not now. Not in my bed, Gwen."

He kissed her full on the mouth. Carefully chosen words didn't stand a chance when softly uttered breaths and quick moans punctuated the air.

He pressed her back. She yielded. It didn't take coaxing or wheedling persuasion. Yearning met yearning, and their bodies entwined.

"Gwen, touch me."

She complied. The bare, oiled chest she'd tried so hard to avoid staring at, lusting after, dreaming about, was slick and hot beneath her palms. His legs were solid, the muscles rippling as he shifted over her. His shorts were satiny. *He* was satin, slick and hot and all the rest of it, pulsing in her hand.

She let him go, only to have him touch her in return, prolonging the time they'd have together.

He lifted her skirt, whispering frank and thrilling words against the trembling skin of her inner thigh, the moistened cotton of her panties. Their bodies did the talking then, a wordless communication of want and hunger, escalating rapidly to an emotional joining of panted requests and instant replies.

"I could say something awful about the thrust of my argument."

She raked his back lightly with her nails. "You do, and I'll groan."

"That sounds good. Feels good too."

"Oh." She gave a startled gasp as she mirrored the pace of his movements, his breathing as rapid and ragged as hers.

"You feel this? Us? There's no other woman who can do this to me, Gwen. Stay with me."

"I'm here." She clung to him, her knees raised to cradle him between, to welcome him.

"Here," he insisted, "And here," plunging into her.

"There," she agreed, biting a corner of her lip until his mouth plundered and claimed it. "Oh, there." Directing, begging, racing with him to the peak. They reached a mountaintop all their own, washed with the colors of the ocean, branded with the flames of the setting sun.

"You feel that?" he asked, his body moving in hers once, twice, until she shuddered to a halt and shook her head. "I think that was an eight-point-five quake."

She opened her eyes, a tardy grin spreading over her kiss-swollen lips. "Don't get smart on me, King."

"On you? Honey, this is the best I get. When I'm with you . . ." He paused, looking down at her heavy lids, the sleepy flush on her cheeks. "I'm the best man I know how to be with you," he whispered starkly. "Don't you know that, Gwen? I'd be a fool to give you up."

It didn't seem quite fair to tell a woman that when sheathed inside her, when she was drugged with desire. He slid out and lay beside her, cheek propped on his hand. "You want to talk about this some more?"

"Define 'talk,'" she murmured guardedly. She felt wasted, depleted, devoured, and, for the first time in far too long, whole. "What did you want to talk about?"

"The only thing that matters. You. Me." He kissed her arm.

"That's two things."

"It can be one. If we want it to be. Tell me what you want."

She just had, in the most brutally honest, uncompromisingly open way. She nodded toward the foot of the bed. "When did you color that?"

He laughed, holding the back of her hand to his chest when she idly lifted it, skimming him, measuring his heartbeat. "One night. One dawn. They all blend together after a while."

She barely raised her chin, looking out the window to the ocean beyond. A thought niggled at the back of her mind. She peered out as if seeking a mast on the water, a distant sail. Then her skin chilled. "And the frame?"

"I mat and frame them myself. I believe in artistic control."

"Like when you color and ink your illustrations."

"All mine." He stroked her hair, her body.

"You look as if you haven't been sleeping," she rebuked him mildly.

"Lot of work to do."

"And?"

"I have to say this? I've been eating my guts out, walking the floor, tying barbed wire around my heart in neat little bows over you. Happy?"

She smiled. "So-so."

"Can I make you happier?" He touched her, familiarly, sexually. He cupped her breast as if it were his to explore, theirs to share. "Or should I say I promised myself I'd never completely lose it over a woman, and by the time I realized how much you meant to me, it was too late."

She pursed her lips and looked at his ceiling. Tiny flecks of metal embedded in the plaster gave the effect of stars twinkling. She laughed at the whimsical, enchanting touch. And held her breath at his carnal one. "You could say that," she said reasonably.

"And what would you say?"

"Now that we're being completely honest? That I want to get married."

He stopped touching her. Gwen held her breath until her heart ached. Then he sat up and walked restlessly to the dresser at the other end of the room.

She wouldn't let her voice quiver. "Is that it? Is that all you're going to say?"

He turned, naked, unashamed, and all male. Four lanky strides brought him to the bedside. The mattress sighed when he sat down. Gwen closed her eyes and held his hand to her abdomen, slowly becoming aware of the small velvet box rasping against the fine hairs there.

Gwen's mouth made a small O. She was afraid to touch it.

He opened it for her.

"A ruby."

"For my red-haired siren."

"Dave."

"Stay with me, Gwen. I mean that in every way possible."

She blinked and put the ring on. The stone wobbled to the other side of her hand.

"We'll size it," he said.

"Only if they do it while we wait. This isn't getting off my finger."

He kissed her playfully, thoroughly. "What if it comes off in the shower?"

"I won't shower."

"No? That's what I planned next."

"You? Planning? What happened to freedom?"

"A man has to look forward to something. Mornings with you. Nights with you. Triumphs, awards."

"Babies?"

"Maybes."

She set the box aside, thinking before she spoke. "Dave? You don't have to marry me. Seriously. You don't have to give me a ring, a fraternity pin, anything. Just promise me one thing."

"What?"

"Every day. Every morning."

He kissed her fingertips, laying their entwined fingers on her breast. "Wouldn't it be more efficient, my efficient lady, if I promised them all right now? Got it out of the way, so to speak?"

"And laughed about it at the same time. I should have known you'd joke about this."

With one easy move he prevented her from storming off. "I laugh with you because I love you. And I'll stay with you, forever, because it's my choice. I love you, Gwen."

"I love you."

The kiss lingered like the dying light over the water, and shimmered like the rising moon.

"If we argue, we'll stick to the rules," Dave promised.

"Charlotte and Robert are having them framed."

"Let's hope they don't bean each other with them at the first sign of renewed hostility."

"Dave?"

"Yes?"

"Stop kidding around and kiss me again."

"Your wish is my command."

She wished on the stars overhead, the lights on the water. "Don't stop loving me."

"Never, my love."

Epilogue

Stuffed with people and noise, the gallery hummed with activity. Gwen inhaled the fragrance of champagne as a waiter wafted a tray of fluted glasses over her head. Dave reached across her easily and picked out one.

He drained it in one swallow, the quicker to retrieve the strawberry floating in the bottom. He presented the fruit to Gwen. She nibbled a bite, knowing how keenly he observed her mouth forming around it, the way the red stained her lips.

"Can I have a taste?" he asked.

"Just one."

He tugged at her mouth with a light sipping kiss. Then Robert's hand smacked his shoulder blade and Charlotte's voice cut through the crowd.

"Bro, I think a star is born."

"That happens every ten minutes in Tinseltown, but thanks all the same." They shook hands warmly, Robert affectionately punching his younger brother's arm.

"I have an idea," Charlotte crooned, "you *must* hear it." She clutched Dave's other arm, her fingernails a brilliant neon green, and led him toward the full-size drawing of Ragnar and his northern lights.

"Now this is just in development," she said, "but tell

me how it hits you. *Ragnar: The Movie.* Yes? Am I right? I see a Conan, a Terminator, and yet sensitive under all those pectorals. A superhero for the nineties. Industrial Light and Magic will handle the aurora bore-us, whatever. We're talking big, Dave, very big."

"The picture or the star?"

"The money." Gwen laughed, tugging her husband away.

They'd eloped to Vegas a week before the showing. The entire ceremony had been tacky, hilarious, and sweeter than she could have imagined. An Elvis impersonator singing "Love Me Tender" had never been in her wedding plans, but, then, neither had Dave.

They lost Robert and Charlotte in the crowd as they mingled their way back to the two large sketches Dave had formally titled *One* and *Two*. They were merely the first in a series, a lifetime's work, in fact.

"Intense but gentle," a spectator announced.

"Tempestuous lines but such controlled effect."

"Passionate and proud and saucy."

"Look at the look on her face."

Gwen colored, Dave tucking her hand in his arm. "They're right," he murmured. "That is one sexy woman."

Under the brim of an enormous hat Charlotte had loaned her, Gwen gave him a warning look. "Thank heaven no one's recognized me."

"That's because they haven't seen your legs," he whispered.

"Hush."

"Such an unusual couple," someone remarked as Dave escorted Gwen in a new direction.

She knew how they looked, so far apart in height, in build, in style. She cherished their differences, so did he. And yet, she knew through the years there would be growth and change. That was natural, that was love. They brought things to each other that neither alone would have ever found.

"In here," Dave said, shuffling her into the gallery office. The noise died instantly as he shut the door. "Think they like 'em?"

He asked so sincerely, she laughed out loud. "They're being snapped up for record prices."

"I knew marrying an accountant would have its rewards."

The door burst open, and the harried gallery owner rushed in. "Sorry. Didn't mean to intrude." She grabbed a price list from her desk and scooted out, stopping on the threshold for one brief command. "Don't forget to say good-bye to the McKenzies, they're buying four."

"Told you so." Gwen laughed lightly when they were alone again. "Shouldn't you be mingling?"

"I want to dance with my wife first," Dave replied, as if dancing in offices was entirely normal. He hummed "Love Me Tender."

Gwen leaned against him, raising her lips to his.

First, she poked him in the nose with her hat.

"Take that thing off. Then take off everything else." His voice half chuckle, half growl, shimmied up and down her skin.

"Oh no. There are some risks you'll never talk me into." She clamped her hand on top of her hat as if staring down a bracing wind. That's what Dave had been, sweeping through her orderly, methodical life.

"You're the hit of the show," he reminded her. "There's a gallery of people out there wondering who my mystery woman is. I haven't thanked you enough for letting me include the sketches."

"You, uh, talked me into it."

He knew as well as she his methods had been strictly dishonorable and thoroughly thrilling. She quivered just thinking of them.

He'd made her a promise, one among many. The sketches would never be sold. Then he'd given them to her as a wedding present, a visible sign of their love.

She let the hat glide to the floor. What was she

hesitating for? She trusted his love; it grew deeper and fuller every day. She trusted their future.

She kissed him, their lips repeating vows pledged over and over again. Her body swayed softly against his. "I can't wait to get back to the house," she whispered.

"There's a full moon."

"And an empty bed."

"A wonderful night for a moondance," he murmured, taking her in his arms once more.

THE EDITOR'S CORNER

What a marvelously exciting time we'll have next month, when we celebrate LOVESWEPT's ninth anniversary! It was in May 1983 that the first LOVESWEPTs were published, and here we are, still going strong, still as committed as ever to bringing you only the best in category romances. Several of the authors who wrote books for us that first year have become *New York Times* bestselling authors, and many more are on the verge of achieving that prestigious distinction. We are proud to have played a part in their accomplishments, and we will continue to bring you the stars of today—and tomorrow. Of course, none of this would be possible without you, our readers, so we thank you very much for your continued support and loyalty.

We have plenty of great things in store for you throughout the next twelve months, but for now, let the celebration begin with May's lineup of six absolutely terrific LOVESWEPTs, each with a special anniversary message for you from the authors themselves.

Leading the list is Doris Parmett with **UNFINISHED BUSINESS,** LOVESWEPT #540. And there is definitely unfinished business between Jim Davis and Marybeth Wynston. He lit the fuse of her desire in college but never understood how much she wanted independence. Now, years later, fate plays matchmaker and brings them together once more when his father and her mother start dating. Doris's talent really shines in this delightful tale of love between two couples.

In **CHILD BRIDE,** LOVESWEPT #541, Suzanne Forster creates her toughest, sexiest renegade hero yet. Modern-day bounty hunter Chase Beaudine rides the Wyoming badlands and catches his prey with a lightning whip. He's ready for anything—except Annie Wells, who claims they were wedded to each other five years ago when he was in South America on a rescue mission. To make him believe her, Annie will use the most daring—and passionate—

moves. This story sizzles with Suzanne's brand of stunning sensuality.

Once more Mary Kay McComas serves up a romance filled with emotion and fun—**SWEET DREAMIN' BABY,** LOVESWEPT #542. In the small town where Bryce LaSalle lives, newcomers always arouse curiosity. But when Ellis Johnson arrives, she arouses more than that in him. He tells himself he only wants to protect and care for the beautiful stranger who's obviously in trouble, but he soon finds he can do nothing less than love her forever. With her inimitable style, Mary Kay will have you giggling, sighing, even shedding a tear as you read this sure-to-please romance.

Please give a rousing welcome to newcomer Susan Connell and her first LOVESWEPT, **GLORY GIRL,** #543. In this marvelous novel, Evan Jamieson doesn't realize that his reclusive next-door neighbor for the summer is model Holly Hamilton, the unwilling subject of a racy poster for Glory Girl products. Evan only knows she's a mysterious beauty in hiding, one he's determined to lure out into the open—and into his arms. This love story will bring out the romantic in all of you and have you looking forward to Susan's next LOVESWEPT.

Joyce Anglin, who won a Waldenbooks award for First Time Author in a series, returns to LOVESWEPT with **OLD DEVIL MOON,** #544. Serious, goal-oriented Kendra Davis doesn't know the first thing about having fun, until she goes on her first vacation in years and meets dashing Mac O'Conner. Then there's magic in the air as Mac shows Kendra that life is for the living . . . and lips are made for kissing. But could she believe that he'd want her forever? Welcome back, Joyce!

Rounding the lineup in a big way is **T.S., I LOVE YOU,** LOVESWEPT #545, by Theresa Gladden. This emotionally vivid story captures that indefinable quality that makes a LOVESWEPT romance truly special. Heroine T. S. Winslow never forgot the boy who rescued her when she was a teenage runaway, the boy who was her first love.

Now, sixteen years later, circumstances have brought them together again, but old sorrows have made Logan Hunter vow never to give his heart. Theresa handles this tender story beautifully!

Look for four spectacular books on sale this month from FANFARE. First, **THE GOLDEN BARBARIAN,** by bestselling author Iris Johansen—here at last is the long-awaited historical prequel to the LOVESWEPT romances created by Iris about the dazzling world of Sedikhan. A sweeping novel set against the savage splendor of the desert, this is a stunningly sensual tale of passion and love between a princess and a sheik, two of the "founders" of Sedikhan. *Romantic Times* calls **THE GOLDEN BARBARIAN** ". . . an exciting tale . . . The sizzling tension . . . is the stuff which leaves an indelible mark on the heart." *Rendezvous* described it as ". . . a remarkable story you won't want to miss."

Critically acclaimed author Gloria Goldreich will touch your heart with **MOTHERS,** a powerful, moving portrait of two couples whose lives become intertwined through surrogate motherhood. What an eloquent and poignant tale about family, friendship, love, and the promise of new life.

LUCKY'S LADY, by ever-popular LOVESWEPT author Tami Hoag, is now available in paperback and is a must read! Those of you who fell in love with Remy Doucet in **RESTLESS HEART** will lose your heart once more to his brother, for bad-boy Cajun Lucky Doucet is one rough and rugged man of the bayou. And when he takes elegant Serena Sheridan through a Louisiana swamp to find her grandfather, they generate what *Romantic Times* has described as "enough steam heat to fog up any reader's glasses."

Finally, immensely talented Susan Bowden delivers a thrilling historical romance in **TOUCHED BY THORNS.** When a high-born beauty determined to reclaim her heritage strikes a marriage bargain with a daring Irish soldier, she never expects to succumb to his love, a love that would deny the English crown, and a deadly conspiracy.

And you can get these four terrific books only from FANFARE, where you'll find the best in women's fiction.

Also on sale this month in the Doubleday hardcover edition is **INTIMATE STRANGERS** by Alexandra Thorne. In this gripping contemporary novel, Jade Howard will slip into a flame-colored dress—and awake in another time, in another woman's life, in her home . . . and with her husband. Thoroughly absorbing, absolutely riveting!

Happy reading!

With warmest wishes,

Nita Taublib

Nita Taublib
Associate Publisher
FANFARE and LOVESWEPT

FANFARE

NOW On Sale
THE GOLDEN BARBARIAN

☐ (29604-3) $4.99/5.99 in Canada
by Iris Johansen

"Iris Johansen has penned an exciting tale. . . . The sizzling tension . . . is the stuff which leaves an indelible mark on the heart." --<u>Romantic Times</u>
"It's a remarkable tale you won't want to miss." --<u>Rendezvous</u>

MOTHERS

☐ (29565-9) $5.99/6.99 in Canada
by Gloria Goldreich

The compelling story of two women with deep maternal affection for and claim to the same child, and of the man who fathered that infant. An honest exploration of the passion for parenthood.

LUCKY'S LADY

☐ (29534-9) $4.99/5.99 in Canada
by Tami Hoag

"Brimming with dangerous intrigue and forbidden passion, this sultry tale of love . . . generates enough steam heat to fog up any reader's glasses."
--<u>Romantic Times</u>

TOUCHED BY THORNS

☐ (29812-7) $4.99/5.99 in Canada
by Susan Bowden

"A wonderfully crafted, panoramic tale sweeping from Yorkshire to Iceland . . . to . . . London. An imaginative tale that combines authenticity with a rich backdrop and a strong romance." -- <u>Romantic Times</u>